LOVE WITH A TWIST

AN ANTHOLOGY OF SHORT STORIES

Edited by
'Doc' David, Jude Jones, Peter Meinertzhagen,
Sarah Milne Das & Tiffany Williams

Oxford
Writing
Circle.

LOVE WITH A TWIST
An anthology of short stories

First published by Oxford Writing Circle Press in 2018

Text & art copyright © Individual contributors
Cover design © Alexander Walker
< www.alexander-walker.co.uk >
Illustrations, pages 3, 28, 39, 45, 58, 72, 80, 86, 112 & 117
© Sophie Temple
Book layout: 'Doc' David

A CIP catalogue record for this book is available from
the British Library

ISBN paperback **978-1-9998832-2-5**
ISBN ebook **978-1-9998832-3-2**

CONTENTS

Dear readers of *Love With a Twist*,

This is not an ordinary collection of love stories.

Rather than tread the familiar ground of love letters, sonnets, and romantic fiction, the writers of the Oxford Writing Circle were tasked to present a twist to the well-worn theme of "love" — or perhaps a twisted version of it.

Whether through showing that the seemingly fundamental need to love or be loved is fraught with suffering and pain or that the concept of "love" can be extended beyond the confines of human desire, the seventeen stories within this collection treat the words "I love you" as being wholly unoriginal.

In the foreword to our last collection, *Oxford's Haunted*, I wrote that the Oxford Writing Circle had cemented itself as a community rich with talent. With this, our third published book, our members show that this was no one-off and that readers can expect more to come in the future.

Merely hours before writing this foreword I learnt that Dennis, the proprietor of Oxford's Albion Beatnik Bookstore, had decided to close the shop's doors permanently. The Albion Beatnik hosted the Oxford Writing Circle's first ever event in February 2015 and since then the shop has felt like the group's spiritual home. I wanted to use this opportunity to thank Dennis for the support and encouragement he has offered us over these past three years and say that the closing of the Albion Beatnik is a huge loss not only to us but to all of Oxford. Dennis, good luck with your future endeavours.

Thanks also to Alexander Walker whose cover adorns the

front of this book (and whose fantastic story made it into this collection); to Sophie Temple whose illustrations make this book as beautiful to look at as it is enjoyable to read; and to this book's editors: Jude Jones, Tiffany Williams, Sarah Milne Das, and 'Doc' David — it wouldn't have been possible without them.

And finally, I ask you, the reader, to throw away that bunch of flowers and scoff down that box of chocolates all to yourself, and embrace an alternative Valentine's Day treat: this is *Love with a Twist*.

Peter Meinertzhagen
Founder, Oxford Writing Circle

LOVE WITH A TWIST

AN ANTHOLOGY OF SHORT STORIES

GLASS SLIPPERS

F E Bradbury

It was meant to be perfect, a fairy tale.

She sat on the stone floor, looked out at her prince's re-treating shape in the doorframe, and tears welled.

She couldn't, mustn't cry.

Strings of chandelier crystal caught the candlelight glim-mering from empty tables and she looked at the vaulted ceil-ing, her feet swelling inside glass heels.

She'd stolen her stepmother's gown, the glass slippers, gone to the commoners' ball at the king's palace, tottering each glass step, biting back screams of pain as heels and toes bled against glass ridges. Contained, she thought. Contained between each stone, between each smile, that first night she'd met him and he'd asked her to waltz in the frozen hall, stone angels frowning from sculpted keystones. She'd faint-ed from pain and cold, and he'd carried her past his parents and shocked guests to gardens and gardens of rose-trellised arbours, leafy aviaries and frothing fountains, and they began to talk for the first time.

He was contained, too, she realised. Contained in expecta-tions, trapped as she'd been, and she sensed their sameness. He'd swiped a spider mid-feast from its web in the walled or-chard, told her the world was like that spider and knelt among the squashed, fallen apples to ask her to marry him.

You're not like them, he'd said, I know it's too soon —

She ran.

He'd followed, faster than she, carrying slippers she'd flung in the gravel for speed.

Chastened, she'd slowed down, feet bleeding.

He'd rescue her, he said, scooping her up when he saw her cut feet. It would be them against the world, its lies and webs. That made him perfect for her, he said, and she for him. She'd said yes — and he'd set her down at the gates.

I must ask my father, he said.

She'd walked home, barefoot, and he'd told his father. She left her stepmother's house behind, carrying with her mildewed books and darned dresses, stepmother and stepsisters howling at her to never return from the top window. The guards wouldn't let her in again at the gilded gates, so she entered through the kitchens.

I'd like the orchard at dusk, with petals and candles everywhere, she'd said later that night.

I must ask my father, he'd replied.

The king forbade the orchard and petals, burnt her books and rags, but allowed candles and his son's choice of bride. The king ordered her fine silks, a strict diet, and the glass slippers returned to her feet, since these were now a symbol of his monarchy's love for its people. She was obliged to wear glass shoes always.

My feet aren't doll's feet, she said at last. These hurt.

I must ask my father, said the prince — and I must ask my father, he said again, when she voiced more. The king refused. You have power, she argued — but I must ask my father, said the prince again. Ask me, she begged — but I can't, he said, you don't understand.

She sat through her days in shawls, in cold rooms, beside

the silent queen who wore silks and gems her husband chose for her. Unable to walk, her future daughter-in-law sat near, shivering and pale, as her hot, reddened feet only seemed to grow and grow in her glass shoes.

I'll die here, she mused.

Months passed. Sparkling wines were delivered to the kitchens. Ivy was twisted between the balustrades. Tables were decked with candelabra, crystal and silver. There came a sweeping dress of ivory flounce and gold brocade that swamped her starving frame.

The night before, she'd stumbled once more through her wedding rituals, practising her bearing, again in glass shoes, as the king demanded. Just past midnight, the king left. She could take no more, and she turned to the prince.

You were supposed to be perfect, he wept, the girl with the glass slippers.

I wouldn't be human, she told him.

I'm so sorry, as he left.

She'd sunk to the floor, but she needed to be stronger than this.

She couldn't, mustn't cry.

She levered the glass shoes from her broken feet, stumbling for the servants' door, for life past the shrieking aviaries of the gardens.

BUZZING

Jude Jones

Whenever he thought I wasn't looking, his eyes lurched out of his head and buried themselves in me. They skimmed over my hair, watched my fingers drumming the edge of my seat, the corner of my mouth as I sipped a cocktail. They followed my bra strap as it escaped down my shoulder, and dove into my cleavage when I moved to correct it. I couldn't help but shiver, and he asked if I was cold. I pulled my cardigan tighter around me. "Yeah, your eyes just alerted me to the fact that I must be." I pointedly buttoned. He laughed at himself, men only ever have one thing on their minds, right? But really he was concerned with my welfare, I must be cold? He slid his chair a little closer with a sly show of caffeine-stained teeth. I finished my drink in three steady glups.

Lucky for me the pub closed and I had to be up early for work in the morning. Unlucky for him, he said. All of a sudden his face was blocking the footpath, unfocused by too many cocktails, and his fingernails were scratching at the palms of my hands. He'd had a really great time this evening. We should do this again sometime. I edged away from him with the excuse of needing to check the bus timetable, but he checkmated me by insisting he should walk me to my stop.

The number 4a bus sealed my doom — a twenty-minute

wait. He suggested a walk through the park to pass the time and I declined, citing the now slightly-swirling pavement and unreliable buses. I went to squint at the timetable again and made the fatal error of tripping over my own feet, right into a bony half-tackling rescue attempt. He warned me to be careful, clumsy! Then he stuck his tongue between my teeth.

Time blurred a bit then. We stumbled away until we found ourselves in a shelter of greyish-green. I could taste my whiskey sours again, mixed with warm saliva and a few stale cigarettes. My ears were flooded with muggy whisperings telling me his thoughts all evening about my dress, my legs, my eyes, my lips, until his mouth found a new home suckered onto my neck while his hands busied themselves with my once-defiant buttons. Occasional thoughts of *why the fuck am I doing this?* replaced themselves with *why the fuck not, I guess*. Then it was all cold hands, hot breath, skirt crawling up and underwear down, and maybe could you just go a little — BAM, fingers in cunt. His nails were too long. I rippled with a stifled groan and he took it as a good sign. I pushed him away, and dropped to my knees. He took it as a very good sign.

I missed my bus, or maybe it was very late. Anyway, we sat in the shelter for a long ten minutes before one came along. He clung to my hand and made me promise to text him when I got home. I promised, and sat on the side of the bus closest to the road so I wouldn't have to wave goodbye again. I pulled my cardigan closer around me and leant my forehead on the greasy window. The world was beginning to straighten up a bit with all the fresh air and my judgement was making gains on me. I pushed it back until the morning and distracted myself with my phone. But he was already there:

`Had a great time already can't wait to see you again soon. Lmk when you get home safe yeah xxx`

I dismissed the notification, and threw myself into bed as soon as I got home without a second thought. My phone was buzzing in my hand as I fell asleep.

`Hey you got home alright last night? Xxx`

I was running late for work again, and tipped the rest of my coffee into a travel mug. My work shoes, drafted into the previous evening's uniform, bounced in a canvas bag against my hip as I half-jogged in my trainers to my bus stop.

`Just checking in again that you werent murdered or something haha =] xxx`

The morning dragged along until lunch time, when I treated myself to a diet lemonade from the machine in the staff room. I'd avoided a hangover, but there was still this juddering, icky feeling sticking to me that I was trying to get rid of. I went for a walk around the town to see if I could air myself out.

`I can see you're not much of a texter lol that's ok. You free tomorrow night? Xxx`

The afternoon dragged too. The promise of the pub with friends was like a light at the end of an ever-extending tunnel of work. "Uhh, I can't believe it's only Wednesday," I heard myself moan to a colleague. I was that desperate for distraction.

`Hey it's almost like your ignoring me haha xxx`

My friend greeted me with a hug and waiting glass of wine. "I was worried you wouldn't show up," she said. "My phone seems to think you hadn't read my messages."

"I saw you'd messaged me, but I didn't want to open the app, sorry. This guy won't leave me alone, and if I looked at your message he'd be able to see I'd been using the app, and..." I waved my hands in circular motions. "Etc. Etc. You get it."

"I get it."

`Did I do something wrong hun? Or are you`

`just that busy lol Xxx`

I explained the previous evening's events, the annoyance that built and built with every notification, and the feeling of intense lethargy that overcame me anytime I thought of opening his messages. I didn't have to explain why things had gone so far the night before. "We've all done it, sometimes you just... make mistakes." Exactly, we sang together, loud enough to cause the people at the next table over to turn their heads.

`Seriously, what's the matter with you? I really really feel like you're ignoring me now. I can see you've been online.`

"Very pushy, isn't he?" Intensely. We agreed together that the best tactic was to pay him no further mind. We checked what would become the final few messages, and his fate was sealed:

`Hello? Ignoring me?`

`Why are you ignoring me? I can see you've been online?`

`Whatever haha sure go ahead and dont bother responding then, see if I care bitch`

I muted my phone, and the sickly sensation in me seemed to disappear with the noise.

My bed was perfectly unmade for me when I got home — pillows thrown and duvet crumpled in just the right way to cradle me as I half-dozed on my phone. My attention was divided between the laptop, balanced on its side beside me, and the profile of the man in front of me. I swiped left without much thought, he hadn't filled in any of his profile properly. I was shown another one, who had only uploaded pictures of his naked torso. I appreciated them for a second, and dismissed him. The next one was promising so I approved his profile and was notified that we were a match. Satisfied with the progress I had made, I turned my attention back to my show until a buzz snapped me back to my phone.

`Hey sexy you ever had a threesome or want to?`

I shut the app down and tossed my phone into a pile of clothes at the end of my bed in protest against his brazen grossness. I stared back at the laptop screen but the words were just skimming over me now. A queasy tremor shuddered its way up from the pit of my stomach and I wrapped myself in my arms to stop it shaking me. I was appalled to feel my cheeks turning red. Was it me?

My phone buzzed again, and I kicked the blanket over it. I held myself tighter, angry that everyone else should be so disappointing, outraged that they were making me pay for it. Stupid, I thought. My phone buzzed again. I buried my face in my pillow and concentrated on the feel of the duvet beneath me. I breathed deep to try and blow the disgust out of me. My phone buzzed again.

And of course, I picked it up.

SHARED INTERESTS

Abigail Vint

"Sorry, how much was that?" His voice was indignant.

Gemma repeated herself in a cautious tone. "£13.50, please."

The man made an audible gasp of shock and shoved the coins he had in his hand back into his wallet, retrieving a £20 note.

She heard him mutter under his breath, "For two beers and shit flavoured crisps," shaking his head as he wandered away.

"Sorry again about the chilli crisps," she called after him, hoping to make up for his disappointment. He didn't turn back but offered a muffled "It's fine."

She had been working the snack bar at the picturehouse in Jericho for a few weeks now and was just getting used to the British way — grumble and moan but carry on. She had known she was going to be a long way from home when she came to the city, but it was the little things that it took some time to get used to.

"Can I help you?" she said, echoing her colleague's "How can I help?" to the next customers in line.

A small voice came from the other side of the counter, but Gemma could not see a face.

"Can I have some sweets please?" the high pitched squeak

came out. Gemma popped up on her tiptoes to look over the edge at a small girl, with braided pigtails, bright brown eyes and sparkling white tiny teeth looking up at her.

"Oh, well, sure. We have a few options..." Gemma saw the girl's eyes widen and her small mouth grow wide.

She hadn't finished her list before a middle-aged, tired-looking man approached the young girl.

"Poppy, there you are! Don't walk off on me like that, sweetheart. We're in a big place and I want to make sure I can see you."

"But Daddy," Poppy protested, "I wanted to get us some sweets."

The man blushed a doting grin, looking up apologetically at Gemma and then back down to his daughter. "Getting us some sweets, are you? Ok, well, let's see if this nice lady can help us."

The interaction pulled at Gemma's heart and she felt, for a moment, envious of the girl and her attentive father.

"Yes, I was just about to tell the young lady what candy we had," Gemma addressed the man, now affectionately resting his hand on his daughter's head.

She went through the list and her little customer chose the chocolatey-est one.

The dad shot Gemma a grateful look. "Thank you very much."

"Of course, no problem. Hope you enjoy the movie."

She let her gaze follow the father and daughter out towards the theatre screens. She wasn't sure how long she'd been staring at them but suddenly a new customer was standing in front of her.

"Oh hi there, can I get you something?" She hoped her friendly voice distracted from the bright red cheeks she could feel burning across her face. How long had this man been standing there waiting for her to serve him?

But he didn't appear to be in a rush. The man stared for a brief second before speaking. "Yes uhhh," he said, staring blankly up at the menu board. "Can I have a Bud, please?"

Gemma couldn't help but notice the deep green colour of his irises as he made direct eye contact with her when he spoke. Without any angst or grumbles, he reached into his wallet for a £10 note.

"Sure thing, anything else?"

"Well, I see you're recommending chocolate bars. Any suggestions?"

Gemma laughed and could feel herself blush again. So he had been standing there for a while. She decided to play along.

"I guess if you have the same taste as a 6-year-old, I'd go with this one," she said. The man gave a loud laugh.

"I hear that's the one the kids are into. If you can't beat 'em, join 'em. I'll take one of those too."

"Good choice." Gemma laughed as she handed him the candy bar. "Anything else?"

The man raised his hand in mock surrender. "I think that'll be all for me."

Gemma took the note from his hand and passed back a few pound coins. She turned towards the next customer, but noticed him lingering for a few moments, before taking his beer and heading towards the theatre.

It was three days later before Gemma had another shift. She only had about a ten-minute walk to get to work along the terraced streets.

The movie house was easy to spot. The sky-blue exterior with the purple cursive lettering was a beacon on the street. From the outside, you could see the neon lights flashing *Screen 1* and *Screen 2*. Even after a recent refurb, it still felt dated but comfortably quirky. And not all theatres had a cosy bar upstairs.

She had barely peeled off her outdoor layers before her co-worker Robb came at her, frantic.

"We need someone to work the bar today. Marie called in sick and Dexter is too young to serve booze on his own. Have you ever worked a bar before?"

She placed a reassuring hand on Robb's shoulder.

"Don't worry — I used to bartend back home. I got this. "

Robb exhaled and clasped his hands together in mock prayer.

"Excellent — you'll do just fine up there then." Before heading back to the main cash register, he turned quickly to add, "Just remember you're in England — don't expect any tips."

She laughed. It had only been a few months but she had learned quickly not to bother with any extra cash when ordering a drink.

"I'll be fine." She headed up the stairs.

The small room at the top of the theatre was empty but welcoming. Gemma was pleased when she got behind the bar to see it had been left in good shape from whoever was working last night.

She was just getting her bearings when she heard footsteps coming up the stairs. The sound of two women's voices grew louder as they approached. The women spent the first 30 seconds at the bar talking animatedly about something that had nothing to do with their order. It took them some time to even acknowledge Gemma behind the bar, and when they did, it was just a quiet nod.

Finally they managed to decide. "Do you do bottles of wine?" one of the woman asked.

Gemma hadn't a clue but tried to be helpful, pulling out a small menu that sat atop the bar. They did, it appeared and so decision made, Gemma went to retrieve the selected bottle, with a couple of glasses.

She could see another figure in her peripheral vision sitting down at a table amongst the antique film paraphernalia that decorated the bar. After the women paid, Gemma went back to wiping down the counter. It was then he approached.

Gemma recognised him immediately. His was the friendliest face she had seen in her time at work. Plus, there he was again, with his wallet in one hand and a £10 note in the other, before he had even ordered.

He started with "Hi," and gave a shy smile.

"Well, hello again!" she exclaimed with a bit too much energy, she thought. "What can I get for you?"

He returned her enthusiasm. "I was thinking of branching out a bit and getting a Peroni," he smiled. "You know, when in Rome."

They both laughed and she heard it for sure.

"Yes, that certainly doesn't sound like an accent from around here."

He raised his greying eyebrows. "Am I that transparent? Guess it takes one to know one."

She laughed. "I wondered when you'd notice mine."

The man didn't ask but simply held out his £10 note even closer to her.

"I've not been here long," she offered, pulling out the Peroni from the small fridge behind the bar.

"Oh no?" he asked, playing with the note in his hand.

"No," she said. "Only been here since September. I'm originally from Toronto."

The man's eyes perked up. "Oh is that right? All the way from America's hat?"

Gemma feigned offense and then corrected him, "I guess you're from Canada's ass then?"

Gemma was impressed with the belly laugh he returned.

"Touché," he replied, grabbing the opened Peroni from the bar. "And you're right. From a city in upstate New York. Lemme guess," he smiled, "You've started a year at some prestigious Oxford college?"

She laughed as he tried to shift into a posh English accent.

"Well, yes I guess you could say that. Worcester College. Just down the road."

She met his eyes. She hadn't noticed they glistened a bit.

When he didn't reply, she got back to business.

"That'll be £5 please."

He paid for the beer but then remained at the bar. Gemma thought for a moment that perhaps she hadn't given him the right change.

"I'm Jeffery, by the way. Most people call me Jeff." His non-beer-holding hand extended across the bar.

"Gemma," she replied, shaking it.

"Thanks, Gemma," he said, his hand hanging on a little longer than Gemma expected. He finally did pull it away and quickly replied, "I should get down to my seat. Movie starts in a few minutes. See you around."

Gemma nodded and teased, "Thanks, Canada's ass."

He walked away from the bar with a small chuckle and gave Gemma a playful wave as he headed towards the theatre.

"Well, I'm not sure you understood the film if you thought it was about ageing superheros. It's a story of redemption."

Gemma stopped wiping the counter to give her full attention to the response.

"Both men were clearly old and tired. It's like, don't superheroes need to retire at some point?" She went back to wiping. "Plus, as if either of them would have the strength, I mean, did you see that fight scene?"

Jeff was shaking his head, laughing but indignant. "They're

superheroes! They have powers beyond our knowledge."

"Well, it didn't seem plausible."

"Of course it's not plausible," Jeff implored. "They have X-Men strength."

Gemma was about to respond in her usual way but a few customers had appeared and she turned her attention towards them.

It had been a few weeks since Gemma and Jeff had met. In that time, they had formed a routine. Jeff would arrive about thirty minutes before the start of a movie and they'd chat about the film he'd seen the day before. She hadn't plucked up the courage to ask him why he was at the theatre every day, but he seemed to not mind watching movies more than once. Perhaps, she thought, he was a professor, gathering information for his classes? Perhaps he was in film and was researching for future roles? This area of Oxford would be a decent place for someone looking to go incognito. There were enough accented voices around that you wouldn't get that many looks if yours didn't fit in, she thought.

Or maybe he was a mature student, taking some sort of sabbatical from his real life to study the classics in Oxford? The classics and every film this picturehouse played, evidently, she laughed to herself.

They seemed to have different tastes in movies but both enjoyed a friendly heated discussion. Last week, she had attempted to get him to fall in love with a romantic comedy set in India with a bunch of retired people without much success.

"They are all finding a new lease on life in this mysterious new place."

He had snorted. "They all sounded like major whiny losers to me. Too cheap to retire to a real destination and too whiny to be around any normal human."

That had made her laugh but it didn't stifle her resolve to

change his mind. She was not surprised that he was now trying to get her to love the physical prowess of a couple of old dudes.

Customers served, she turned back to her fellow movie critic.

"So, what's on the Jeff viewing schedule tonight?"

His face winced before he answered.

"Well, unfortunately, they only had tickets left for the latest redo of a Disney romance."

Gemma slapped her hands together as she made an *ooooooooohhhhhh* sound before nodding in approval.

"I REALLY want to see that! Such a classic. And the remake is supposed to be so good!"

Jeff shook his head, one side of his mouth rising up.

"Based on our past history, a recommendation from you does not mean it's going to be good for me."

Gemma turned away from the bottles of beers she was shelving to face him.

"I'll have you know many people like my movie recommendations. You're just too old to appreciate them." She stuck her tongue out at him before bending back down to pick up the empty cardboard boxes.

Jeff didn't reply but Gemma did notice him do that thing with his face he'd sometimes do: he pressed his lips together in reflection and his green eyes sparkled a bit more than normal.

They were quiet for a few moments before Gemma heard him stand and start to gather his things.

"Well, here goes nothing. I look forward to discussing this with you more tomorrow, America's Hat."

Gemma rolled her eyes and threw him a cheeky smile.

"Sounds good, Canada's Ass. Gonna be a tear jerker. Make sure you take a tissue."

She turned back to her work, catching him pause at the top of the stairs, before he made his way back down and into the theatre.

It hadn't taken long for Gemma to land the job at the picture-house in Oxford.

"Well, it looks like you've got some good customer experience. Have you ever worked at a picturehouse before?" the manager Michelle had asked.

"No, but I do like going to the movies."

Her enthusiasm paid off and Michelle offered her the job on the spot. She had been good to Gemma for the past few months, making her transition away from home that much easier. Plus, working was part of her usual routine..

Gemma couldn't really remember a time she didn't have a job. She had had to start earning money as soon as she was able. Being an only child raised by a single mother had its benefits — close bond, 100% attention — but there were also the downsides — her money situation was always tight.

She had started waitressing when she was thirteen, at a diner just on the outskirts of town, alongside her best friend, Macy, and Macy's mother. It was her first experience with financial freedom — making her own money to buy what she wanted. But she also felt the pride of helping out. After her first paycheque, she decided to take her mother out for dinner. She remembered being so proud to give her mother something. And she remembered her mother discreetly wiping her eyes when Gemma had asked for the bill.

Her father had never been in the picture and Gemma wasn't really sure that mattered. She had a full childhood, growing up surrounded with extended family, including aunts and uncles. Her mother had never really said a bad word about her father but he very much was not part of their lives. Whenever Gemma asked, her mother merely said that she had wanted Gemma all to herself. And her father was simply a means to an end.

Gemma was so close with her mother that she was happy to accept this as an answer. She had only missed him on those times the world forced her to — Father's Day, Daddy-Daughter dances, bring your kid to work day.

But otherwise, her and her mom had done alright.

When Gemma left Toronto to come to Oxford, it had been a teary goodbye. She was worried about her mother just as her mother was worried for Gemma. Both part of a mutual concern society.

But Gemma had been doing well, enjoying school, appreciating a bit of freedom, but also eager to feel more financially secure. The picturehouse job had done the trick.

Now she was counting money in the till when Michelle appeared beside her.

"So Gemma, how you getting on? Robb tells me you're doing wonders in the bar." Michelle was leaning against the doorframe, eyes attentive towards Gemma, her body, relaxed, casually playing with an elastic band.

"Yeah, I think it's going pretty well. The bar is working for me, I'm quite used to it."

"Well, customers seem to like you, so you must be fitting in just fine. Especially that old guy."

Gemma turned to look at Michelle, confused.

"Old guy? You mean Jeff?"

"Yeah." Michelle started to lift the recycling bin full of empties. "Never seen him before until you arrived."

Gemma shot her a puzzled look, then continued counting change, unsure how to respond. Michelle did not say anything else nor make any suggestion that there was anything more to her comment.

"Any more empties?" was her next line, and Gemma simply

shook her head. Gemma turned back to the till, the idea about Jeff still rolling around in her brain.

He was there again the next day when she started her shift. Coffee in hand, he had chosen the corner table today, sipping and reading a free pamphlet he had picked up from the large brochure shelf at the end of the bar.

"Morning," she chirped cheerfully, giving him a small wave before assessing the state of the tables. They were all a mess, with glasses and water stains scattered around. Night staff must have been run off their feet, she thought.

"Good morning," his low, gentle voice answered. "Thought I'd try a matinée today."

"I see that," Gemma said, squirting the spray bottle across a set of tables.

"I'm not usually a fan of cartoons, but, this new one doesn't look too bad. Have a bit of a soft spot for the lead actor, or at least, the actor voicing the lead role."

Gemma's face twisted and she let out a laugh.

"That guy? Wow, wouldn't have pegged you as a fan of him. Doesn't he always freak out at the paparazzi?"

"That's why I like him," he replied. "Doesn't put up with any shit from anyone."

Jeff raised his coffee cup towards Gemma in a 'cheers' type fashion and then took a big slurp.

Gemma shook her head as she gave the last table a good swipe.

"Whatever, old man nerd."

Jeff face mocked shock. "Who you calling old? Age gets us all, little lady. Time waits for no-one."

Gemma waved her dirty cloth towards him and he just grinned, staring at her, she noticed, as she walked back towards the bar to check if the glassware was well stocked.

This went on for a few weeks. Jeff would come to the theatre, every day, and would either be waiting there for Gemma when she started or arrive in the middle of her shift. He became a comfortable part of her day, just like the familiarity of the theatre.

Her co-workers, while well-meaning, seemed to worry unnecessarily about Jeff.

"I'm just glad he doesn't speak to me," the sharp-tongued Lila snapped one morning. "Bloody Americans and their blah blah blah. Just order your drink, man, and get on with it."

Gemma let out a small laugh but felt a strong urge to defend him.

"Hey, he's just being friendly! And obviously, he doesn't know that many people." Gemma actually had no idea how many people he knew, but she didn't want Lila to know that. Perhaps he did have a lot of friends in the area? But wasn't it strange, then, that he wouldn't at least bring someone along once in a while?

Gemma was shaken out of her own thoughts by a burst of cold air from the outside as a group of teenagers came tumbling through the door.

Lila served them with her usual non-cheer and then turned back to Gemma.

"Yeah, well, there's probably a good reason for that."

"You're not being fair," Gemma continued. "I mean, he's just a guy who likes to go to the movies and enjoys chatting about it."

"Sure, right, but discussion with only you? Do you not see how he seems to always come to movies when you're on shift? Like he knows your schedule or something?"

Gemma couldn't deny the pattern there. She had simply thought he had talked to her more often because the other staff were not as chatty as she was. Perhaps it was something else.

She turned her back on Lila and ignored her question. "I've got to grab a few more bags of crisps from upstairs. I'll be back right back," Gemma said, hoping she had turned from the conversation in time to hide the perplexed look on her face.

That afternoon, when Jeff arrived, she suddenly felt more self-conscious. She had imagined, being upstairs, that the rest of the team couldn't hear the conversations between herself and Jeff. Now, after what Lila had said, she was certain these chats weren't as private as she'd thought.

"Good morning," boomed Jeff.

"Hi," was all Gemma offered back. She saw in his eyes that he was puzzled by her response.

"You ok?"

"Yep, yep thanks I'm fine," she said, keeping her head down, and grabbing a handful of change from the register to count it.

She could sense Jeff still standing in front of the bar, but she didn't look at him. She wondered if he would order something or how long he would just stand there. A few cars rumbled past, breaking the silence that now engulfed the room. Gemma noticed she had never been in the bar with Jeff when it was so quiet. His fingers made a quick tapping noise as he rapped them on the bartop.

"I'll just have a diet coke today, thanks, Gemma." His voice had turned more formal. He didn't always use her name but she felt the air of closeness they had built over the last few weeks get sucked out of the room.

"Sure," she said. "Of course." Gemma heard her own voice rise an octave and become more customer-service friendly.

The ice clinked into the glass, echoing loudly into the room that felt more vacant than Gemma had ever experienced. A motorcycle zoomed past. The sound of the drink rushing through the tap drowned out the muffled voices that were filtering from the main entrance downstairs up into the bar.

Gemma caught Jeff's eye, almost by accident, and gave a terse smile before looking back out towards the shushing tap.

"Gemma, are you sure you're ok?"

The voice that emerged from Jeff was not the same confident, cheerful one she had become accustomed to over the past few weeks. It was disconcerting to hear him speak that way and she jerked her head up to face him.

"Um, yes, sure. I'm fine. Just busy today." Another forced smile and she hoped that her discomfort didn't show too much.

"Ok," was all he offered back but Gemma could tell that she hadn't succeeded in hiding it from him.

He placed £2.50 on the counter and thanked her for the drink. He turned away, and then paused. His back to her, he said, "You know, I think I'll just take a look at the snack bar downstairs, see what they might have for today's movie."

Gemma froze, squeezing her hands into fists to propel herself to speak. She had wanted to be honest with him, tell him that she wasn't ok. That she had so enjoyed their discussions. That she felt close to him, in a way she couldn't quite place or explain. That she was sorry, that it was not him, it was not her, it was *them*. They had made her question what *this* was.

But she didn't say any of that. She just stared at his back.

Then he turned, looked at her, hesitated before he spoke, and simply said, "Take care, Gemma. I'll see you next time."

Jeff turned, not waiting for a reply, and headed back down the stairs towards the theatre screens. Gemma was left in the bar now echoing with the sounds of vehicles passing by and patrons from the lobby below. She slammed her one hand down on the counter and thrust the change into the other, not quite sure where this all went next.

Jeff had wanted to tell her right then and there what he had been waiting to tell her since the day she sold him that chocolate bar. He had hoped he would have more time, more time to actually get to know her better, share more details about their lives, get her to really like him before he told her.

But then hadn't he been waiting all her life? And now, just as he had gotten close enough, he couldn't do it.

And so he left. He left the bar and walked down the stairs, towards the movie he didn't care about and away from his only daughter.

THE MOTH

Emma M Bokaldere

I see her in my dreams every night, sitting on a bench in front of a slender tree.

The scene is emanating a sort of gentle glow. Darkness everywhere else.

I see her in my dreams every night,

sitting on a bench in front of a slender tree. She is looking at her hands resting in her lap. Her hair is obscuring her face. A strand has detached and is drifting to the ground. The scene is emanating a sort of gentle glow. Darkness everywhere else.

I see her in my dreams every night,

sitting on a bench in front of a slender tree. She is looking at her hands resting in her lap, palms open, upwards. Her hair is obscuring her face. (I wish I could see her face.) A strand has detached and is drifting to the ground. The scene is emanating a sort of gentle glow. Darkness everywhere else.

I see her in my dreams every night,

sitting on a bench in front of a slender tree. She is looking at her hands resting in her lap, palms open, upwards. Her hair is obscuring her face. A strand has detached and is drifting to the ground. The scene is emanating a sort of gentle glow. Darkness everywhere else. I am standing a few metres away. I cannot move. I could never move in this dream.

I see her in my dreams every night,

sitting on a bench in front of a slender tree. A birch tree, much like the one in the garden. She is looking at her hands resting in her lap, palms open, upwards. Her hair is obscuring her face. (I must have imagined it a thousand times over.) A strand has detached and is drifting to the ground. The scene is emanating a sort of gentle glow. Darkness everywhere else. But then, nothing else matters. I am standing a few metres away. I cannot move. I could never move in this dream. The only dream I'll ever dream, maybe. Definitely the only dream I'll ever need.

I see her in my dreams every night,

sitting on a bench in front of a slender tree. A birch tree, much like the one in the garden. She is looking at her hands resting in her lap, palms open, upwards. Her hair is obscuring her face. (Sometimes it seems like she knows I'm here.) A strand has detached and is drifting to the ground. The scene is emanating a sort of gentle glow. Darkness everywhere else. But then, nothing else matters. I am standing a few metres away. I cannot move. I could never move in this dream. The only dream I'll ever dream. The only dream I'll ever need. A haven away from the relentlessness of waking life.

This morning, I woke in cold sweat, a lump of dread in my chest.

It was only when I was boiling an egg for breakfast, watching it roll around in the water, white and smooth and featureless, that I realised why.

She looked up.

FLOWERS

Ashley Thorpe

The last time you brought me flowers guilt was dripping like dew. You wore a laboured smile as you opened the door to our home. You thought you'd purchased true English bluebells – my favourites. But I guess both of us had been deceived that day. The Spanish variety may be reminiscent of our own but there is a difference. *Hyacinthoides hispanica* has broader leaves, a paler flower, and there's no sweetness to its scent. It's quite different from *Hyacinthoides non-scripta*. Not many people know the real thing when they see it, grasp it in their hands. You didn't.

A dozen years is time enough to know someone's habits if not their mind, and the waning hours are most revealing despite the dark of night. With each passing minute lies were flowing from your tongue, oozing from your pores. You spoke with the truth orbiting your head but never quite burning its way through. Two nights later I was driving away from you.

This time when you visit me the guilt you bring is a humid storm. I don't remember seeing you cry before, even when you begged me to stay. You realise now what's been lost. You want my forgiveness but there's nothing more I can say.

You utter your apologies that fall on deaf ears, and a dumb mouth. You place more 'bluebells' over my head and step back making a sign of the cross to admire your work. The last time you brought me flowers I had hands to feel and sense to smell. But even now, I see.

LIGHTHOUSE ROCK

Richard Edwards

"No one visits Lighthouse Rock," said the fisherman.

"But where is it?"

"Just about there, I'd say. But no one visits."

Iason followed the fisherman's pointing finger. As far as he could tell, the patch of darkness the man jabbed his finger at was no different to the rest of the night. He could hear sounds coming from that general direction — the roar and spray of an angry tide — but then, the same could be said no matter which direction he turned.

"Why do you want to go out there, anyway?" The fisherman rolled his tobacco around his mouth, squeezing the question through the gaps in his teeth.

"It has to be dark tonight."

The fisherman regarded the void.

"I'd say there's not much worrying to be done on that count."

"Not right now, but if the keeper ignites his light…" Iason grappled with the enormity of the problem. He waved his hands dramatically, buying time, while the fisherman frowned at him.

At last, Iason grabbed the fisherman's shoulders. "*They* won't end up together!"

"Who won't?"

Again, Iason waved. "*They*. Everyone."

The fisherman had more questions, but Iason was already moving away, taking an experimental step into the darkness. Behind him, the fisherman's lantern burned by his tackle box and illuminated a small patch of land around the pair. Until now it had been Iason's guiding light, a yellow north-star marking his destination. Now he moved with nothing more than his faith in the stone beneath his feet.

"Have you been out here in the day?" called the fisherman.

"No!"

"Then you'll want to be careful of the rope bridge. It's a real nightmare to cross."

Iason faltered. He turned to look over his shoulder at the old man.

"There's a rope bridge?"

"Between the pier and Lighthouse Rock. How else did you expect to get out there?"

"I... Didn't think it through."

"No, you don't have the look of a man who plans ahead. Otherwise you'd have brought a light."

"Can I borrow yours?"

The fisherman looked at it. A wave broke against the rocks beneath him, sending droplets of saltwater high into the air. They lingered in the yellow light while the decision was made.

Eventually — "No."

"Please? The Agency will thank you for your service."

"Oh, this is for the *Agency*?" said the fisherman, perking up a little bit. Iason nodded.

"That changes everything!"

"So I can have it?"

"For a price."

Pherenike yawned. He enjoyed it so much he did it again. The third yawn wasn't nearly as satisfying. He didn't attempt a fourth.

He contemplated pressing the button, but it was on the counter several metres away. His arm was not up to the task, not unless his legs were willing to help with the effort. For now an alliance was out of the question because Pherenike was drunk.

Not outrageously so. He could still tell shapes apart, and the world hadn't yet descended into that spinning blur that so often slams into the next morning through a short, darkened tunnel of amnesia. Only his legs had gone, and they always went early these days. After the second hour they'd become no more useful than two sticks of jelly.

The almost empty bottle of whisky sat by the wheels on his chair. The cap — a twist-and-release affair for a drink-and-forget thing — was lost to the shadows. He'd transferred most of the liquid to his stomach and the smell to his breath. Now only a few fingers of amber remained for tomorrow's rations.

Pherenike glanced out of the window, at the pitch black night sky. Who could say when midnight might be?

He took another swig, feeling fire, delighting in the burn. The flavour was there somewhere, but Pherenike's sense of taste had gone the way of his legs.

To buy time, to silence the small voice of obligation, he pulled open the drawer where he kept the manifest. The red letter, holy Manifest, may it guide and protect us all. Never take an action without consulting it — never divulge the contents to an outsider — venerate it, hold it dear, drop to your knees and *praise* it.

Pherenike picked at the sauce stain on this one. He'd had this month's manifest for less than twelve hours and he'd already used it as a plate, a fly swatter and a table-leg-stabiliser, in an order that would upset most people.

He flipped to page one, where the dates and times of the different cargos were outlined, along with the name of the clerk who'd prepared the document. The signature was new to Pherenike, the looping, enthusiastic letters spoke of a junior given his first assignment. Pherenike read the name and wondered who *Iason* was.

Not that it mattered. There was the official stamp at the top of the page. A red circle showed the three discs of creation — the mortal realms, the skies above, the fires below — and the grand ocean that connected them all. Pherenike felt an enormous sense of pride whenever he saw the tiny smudge of ink that represented his lighthouse, although it had never been a cure for loneliness. Only the drink eased that pain.

Not that any of this mattered to Iason. This seal proved Iason spoke with the full authority of the Agency.

He spun a small clock until it faced him. Radium green dials stood out in the darkness. The time was seven thirty, minus a few seconds. Pherenike didn't need to check the date. This was day one of a new manifest.

The first two ships were scheduled to go out at eight. He checked their contents, their destination, their proposed shipping route. Then he did a quick bit of maths, adjusting their time of departure by the time it took for two ships of their size to get to him. Slowed by the storm. Slowed by the inevitable last minute cargo. Jobs like this one inevitably had more than they planned for.

He had time. To sober up, he supposed, or, and this proved tempting, to spend drinking instead. Somewhere along the line he knew he'd have to commit to one plan or the other, but for now he lived in limbo. Both futures were full of glorious possibilities.

Iason made his way through the darkness. The rope bridge left him feeling sea-sick, and now he stood on Lighthouse Rock he took the time to steady himself. The lantern he'd bought was lost to the waves — money he wouldn't see again, but it had brought him some of the way. That alone made it worth the cost.

He felt for something to steady himself against and found nothing but empty space. His hands disappeared into the darkness whichever way he turned. The experience was a disorientating one, and he collapsed to his hands and knees, feeling the wet stone beneath him.

He retched. Vomited. Retched again and felt a wave of relief that he'd had such a small breakfast.

A wave of salt water hit him. He clung on desperately, dimly aware that the water filling his mouth, his nostrils, and his left ear tasted faintly of toast, eggs and bacon.

With the wave gone and his stomach empty, Iason stood again. The Lighthouse loomed somewhere up ahead. Even though his eyes were useless he could sense it, an invisible titan of stone and glass. With the sound of the rope bridge creaking behind him as his only signpost, he forged on until things felt different.

The rain had changed — there wasn't any.

This sudden absence told him he stood in the shadow of the Lighthouse. When he looked — his eyes hurting with the strain — he could make out a patch of sky that wasn't quite as dark as the rest of the world.

He stumbled toward it, cursing when he stubbed his toes against the jagged rock, calling out in pain whenever he tripped, scraping the skin from his hands. Dark patches of blood marked his progress.

And then he was up against the Lighthouse. He ran his fingers along the brickwork, searching for any sign of a door.

He'd taken twenty paces, maybe thirty, it was hard to tell, when his hand brushed up against a length of wood.

A splinter embedded itself in his forefinger. He didn't care. He pushed up against the door and found the handle by bruising his hip. A quick turn, a click, and a portal of light grew, sliding horizontally across, revealing a warm and yellow world. Iason tumbled inside, allowing the relief to drive him to his knees.

His nostrils flared once, sensing some deeply disagreeable odour. But then it faded, replaced by the gentle scent of wild flowers.

Candles flickered on every wall. Crates and barrels filled the room, although they were piled in such a way as to leave a clear path to the first step of the central staircase. It pulled upward, twisting away, and although shadows filled every step, it never fell into complete darkness. The pattern of candles repeated along its walls — hundreds of specks of light joining forces to create a grand, sweeping army.

Iason gave himself some time to let his eyes adjust. Trying to climb the stairs in a blind daze was a recipe for disaster, one that would leave him with even less skin on his knees.

As soon as he was able he took the first step, crawling up one at a time, his face turned down, away from the overwhelming light of the candles. At first only one in four had been lit but, as he drew closer to the top, more and more were burning. About halfway up there weren't enough places to attach candles to the wall and Iason found himself crawling through a tunnel of fire. Candles of all shapes, sizes and smells guided his way.

The resulting mixture was less than pleasant. But Iason carried on, taking great care not to stray too close to the open flames. If he caught fire he'd have a hard time stopping the Lighthouse keeper from pushing that button.

Pherenike heard the coughing long before Iason reached him. It bounced around the staircase, heralding the arrival of an asthmatic. Pherenike recognised that strange quality that a cough gets when it comes from deep within the lungs and is forced through a rapidly narrowing windpipe. He'd heard it before — usually whenever he lit the scented candles.

They were an important part of making the Lighthouse habitable. Without them, the only scent was the stench of seaweed and barrelled fish. The only downside was the effect the sickly perfumes had on visitors. Even the healthiest lungs struggled through the last few steps.

Pherenike spun his chair until it faced the doorway, and then he span a bit too far. Instead of correcting his mistake he let the chair continue on its merry way. There was the far side of the room, there was the desk with the manifest, there was a window, and then there was the door again.

He slammed his feet down. He stopped, but the world moved on.

"Ugh," he said as the whiskey did its best to come back up and say hello.

There came a cough from the otherside of the door, and then a desperate rattling of the handle. Both sounds fell away, leaving nothing but silence, which was interrupted shortly after by a weak knocking.

"Let me..." *wheeze*, "...in."

Pherenike squinted. A key took shape, jutting out of the keyhole. Brass against brass and very difficult to see, even when sober. He smiled, pleased at how effectively he'd brought the world into focus.

Another knock.

With a small exclamation, Pherenike bounded to his feet, intending to stride toward the door. But, his concentration broken, his vision blurred and he staggered to one side. He followed the momentum, turning as he went, until he crashed back into the chair he'd left moments before.

He pulled himself up, struggling against the combined motion of the chair and the booze. "Who is it?" he called, still not quite on his feet.

"Iason!" Another cough, a slight pause, and then, "from the Agency!"

"I'm not drunk!"

"I didn't say… Please. Just open up…"

Pherenike drifted toward the door. Visitors to the rock were unheard of, especially ones claiming to be from the Agency. His mind raced through the possibilities, barely staying on one long enough to form a fully thought before hopping off to the next in a long line of increasingly unlikely suspicions.

What if an inspector knew he was drinking on the job? What if he'd already lost his job and this man was his replacement? What if sabotage? That one didn't get any more specific. It didn't need to be. Just what if sabotage?

He committed himself to a plan of action. He would stall, and hope the situation resolved itself before he needed to do anything. Step one; don't let this visitor in.

"How do I know you're who you say you are?"

"I wrote the manifest. It'll have my signature on it."

Pherenike sighed, partly in relief, partly in terror. He knew, without needing to check, that he'd find Iason's name there, which meant his claims of being from the Agency may have some weight behind them. "Give me a moment to check."

A soft thud rattled the door. "Please hurry…" Iason spoke with a desperation whose roots ran much deeper than the overwhelming scent of the candles.

Pherenike stomped in place, hoping to give the impression he was moving to the desk. Then he stomped again, simulating the walk back. "What did you say your name was?"

"Iason!"

"And your surname?"

"That won't be on the manifest." Iason coughed. "I can tell you there are two ships coming out tonight. They can't be allowed to leave the bay."

That was enough to give Pherenike pause.

"Why not? Ships have been going out for thousands of years, and not a single one has ever been stopped."

Iason didn't reply straight away. The silence was just long enough for Pherenike to begin worrying — what if the scent and smoke of the candles were too much? He reached for the key but stopped when he heard Iason cough once and then, in a shaky voice, say:

"I fucked up."

Pherenike opened the door. No one from the Agency ever admitted to a mistake. Discovering what had brought Iason to the Lighthouse was worth any price.

Really, the problem came down to the letters A and B. That's what Iason said when he finished coughing. Pherenike had installed him in a chair next to his own, and then gingerly lowered himself until the swivel chair took his weight. He gripped the desk, determined not to spin so much as a single degree.

"Artemis and Basileus. Those are the ships," Iason said, tripping over his own words in the rush to explain. Pherenike's hand still lingered dangerously close to the button that would ignite the Lighthouse and steer the ships to safety. He licked his lips. "A and B."

"I don't understand."

"Cargo procedure is all laid out in the manifest. Surely you can see where this is going?"

Pherenike's eyes flicked to his manifest. "Truth be told," he drawled, "I never read the bit about the cargo. Just the dates and times I need to press this."

Iason flinched as the Lighthouse keeper waved a hand over the button, watching it stray close to disaster. It was all he could do not to dive forward and pull Pherenike away, but he worried about accidentally hitting the button during the scuffle. All it would take was a single second and they'd be on the path to an inevitable disaster.

His nerves jangled. The faces of all the couples filled his mind. He'd personally vetted them all, a task that had taken years. And then he'd ruined it all with a stupid assumption.

"When I worked with the passengers they had names. But the boarding passes had a unique ID for each of them, and they all ended with either an A or B. I thought that was to do with the ships."

"Artemis and Basileus," said Pherenike.

"Exactly."

"But they aren't?"

Shaking his head, Iason went on. "It was my order, though. I got it wrong. If it had an A it went aboard the -"

"Basileus."

"What? No, of course not. The As boarded the Artemis. Basileus has the Bs."

"Right, right. That makes sense" Pherenike shifted his leg, pushing the empty bottle further under his desk. "So what went wrong?"

"So what went wrong?"

"I started loading tomorrow's shipment today. Same again, two ships -"

"Let me guess. Actaeon and... Bellerophon?"

"Not even close." Iason jumped, twisting to look upstream. He thought he'd heard a foghorn in the darkness. "Look. Promise me you won't press that button."

"I have to. It's my duty. Unless you can convince me, I suppose, but that's going to be difficult."

"Virgil and Vulcan. Those were the ships. V and V, but all the cargo was still labeled A and B."

"You mean to say the Artemis and Basileus have the wrong cargo?"

"It's worse than that. Some of the cargo will be right, some of it will be wrong. I can't recall the ships, not in this weather. They can't see any flags, and the bells we'd ring will be drowned out by the storm."

"But if the Lighthouse isn't lit..."

"Then the captain will have no choice but to hold position in the darkness. In the morning you'll raise the right flags and send them back to port to get this sorted."

Iason nodded. Then, his plan outlined and his fate firmly in Pherenike's hands, he slumped.

The lighthouse keeper closed his eyes. He needed to think, and Iason was staring at him in a very off-putting way. The man radiated intensity.

Ultimately, his decision came down to one simple fact. It wasn't his problem.

He reached for the button. Iason leapt for him, shoving him to the ground, his fists balled.

The two men were still fighting when the Artemis struck Lighthouse Rock. The sound of rending metal filled the few small moments of peace the storm left.

Both froze, mid-grapple, Iason's hands wrapped around Pherenike's throat, the Lighthouse keeper's knee pushing down hard on the other's chest.

Niether had counted on the ships being foolhardy enough to run the gauntlet of sharp

Pherenike made it to the window first. He stood, frozen in terror, staring down at the corpse of the Artemis. The light from the spilled cargo banished the night and lit the chaos below.

Thousands of shining globes were falling out of the ship. Some rolled across Lighthouse Rock, coming to rest in the craggy landscape. Four or five managed to resist the constant waves, but the majority were pulled out to sea. There some floated and some sank, miniature suns in a dark blue sky, surrounded by the white clouds of the seafoam.

Iason couldn't say how he managed to get down the stairs without falling, but one minute he was scrabbling toward the button, and the next he was down by the Artemis. He grabbed the first sphere he came to, his bare skin brushing the bubbling, golden surface. There was a flash of intense pain and he pulled away, cursing.

That was when the Basileus hit the Artemis. This time there was an explosion — fingers of orange flame reached into the sky, lightning cracked and, for one moment, the whole scene was perfectly illuminated.

There was the city in the distance. The gleaming towers looked even more majestic in the darkness — the imagination filling in all the tiny details. Pure white marble, brilliant golden rooftops, arcing gemstone roads tracing the sky.

The river flowed from that city, through the farmlands to Lighthouse Rock, but it went further still, out into the ocean.

And beyond that... Pherenike could see it more clearly than ever. There was the edge of the world, where the water rushed off the cliff and fell into eternity.

The light died, and all he could do was watch as the cargo raced toward the edge.

It was three days later. Pherenike had traded the bottle for a hotdog. Iason's Agency uniform was gone, replaced by faded denim jeans and an ill-fitting t-shirt. He wore a thick coat over that and he'd wrapped a scarf tightly around his neck. It was colder here, and this was what they called summer. He didn't think he'd ever get used to it.

All around them life went on in a screaming cacophony of engines and voices. This new city was awake.

"I still don't think they should have fired me," Pherenike said around mouthfuls of bread and meat.

"If anything, the captains should share the blame, too. What made them think they could make it in the darkness?"

"Maybe they lost their jobs, too. We'll never find out, and speculation isn't going to get us back up there, is it?" Pherenike pointed beyond the clouds, to where Lighthouse Rock stood at the junction between their worlds.

"You need to accept some of the responsibility, you know. You were drunk on duty that night."

"Correction. I was drunk on duty *every* night. You got me caught."

Iason wasn't listening. His attention had been drawn away by a couple walking, hand in hand, deep in conversation.

"But look at them..." Iason pointed at a couple sitting on a park bench. "They're not supposed to be together. That's Tammy Fletcher and Gaius Aurellius, designations 2114CE-USA-11902-A and 643BCE-ROME-12128-A."

"And?

"They were supposed to live two thousand years apart. Where's Gary Parker and Quintina Cassianus? Where are their Bs?"

"Somewhere else." Pherenike finished his hotdog in one, greedy bite. "Maybe some*when* else."

"I don't understand it. They'll never know their soulmate, but they look..."

"Happy?"

"Yes. Why? We know they're not meant to be together." Iason turned away, looking across at the hot dog cart run by Terry Whitmore, who Iason knew for a fact wasn't supposed to be alive for another sixty four years. He wore a wedding ring. "And him. He's found someone, too."

"Bundling the souls up in little pairs, labelling them A and B, and unpacking them together when they arrive, it's neater, I'll admit that much. But maybe it doesn't matter."

"We had a system. It's worked for a thousand worlds."

"This world implies soulmates don't work. It's in turmoil compared to the others but the humans have found happiness anyway."

"But every A has a B..." Iason tried one last time, and felt himself fall silent at the sight of another couple — both Bs, both inhabiting bodies that weren't intended for them, both at least a hundred years out of time. They had a child. They had their hands in each other's pockets. They had smiles.

Pherenike put a hand on Iason's shoulder. "Face it. We broke the system. We crashed two ships full of souls, and yes, we lost our jobs. But look around you. Earth turned out okay."

Across the road, Terry Whitmore sold another hotdog. The person who bought it walked away, texting someone. Iason watched as she passed by, stealing a glance at her phone. She'd signed the message with a heart.

He sighed.

"What do you want to do now?" Pherenike asked.

Iason shrugged. "I haven't given it much thought. What are your plans?"

"I thought I might start living my life. Get out there. See the sights this world has to offer. Meet people. Who knows what might happen?" The lighthouse keeper smiled. "I might even find my soulmate."

MRS. NICK CARMICHAEL

Lyndsay Wheble

In biology this morning I wrote, 'Mrs Nick Carmichael,' on the bottom corner of my hand-out. God knows why. We all sit nit-close in that class and it always makes us a bit wild. Alice was nervous about going out with Jamie Sommers on Friday, so Janine grabbed her arm and scribbled 'Alice 4 Jamie' in biro onto her skin and encircled it in a shaky love heart. Alice was bright red and twisting away, laughing loudly so that everyone turned to see. Zoë drew a sketch of herself straddling Kevin Lowell, so I chose Nick Carmichael at random from the class-room's front row. I scribbled his name as mine in pencil and encircled it with stars. I was laughing like everyone else but must have done it too quietly as Janine seized on it as *something*. She looked at me wolfishly and was about to lay in when Mrs Wright shouted that it was only seven weeks until our exams, so to pipe down and get on with our work.

After lunch there was a folded-up bit of card with a heart on it in my backpack, from 'Nick,' with 'dirty, sweaty love.' I'd know Janine's handwriting anywhere. I bundled her aside in the corridor between maths and PE and begged her not to spread it, giggling so much that Fanta came out of my nose. She pursed her lips and flashed her eyes at me and immediately, it was clear — this gossip was a carrot or a stick, depending on how she felt that day. Hers alone to say at the wrong moment: *Oh look, its Nick — do you remember that time you practically jumped him in biology?* Something for her to keep in hand. I took a deep breath and leapt in.

"Please don't tell, Janine, you could ruin me! Yes, I'm an idiot. Yes, I really owe you. Yes, you have great tits. Yes, let's go out with Dan and Ian on Friday. I love you, Janine," I said, stretching the latter words out like chewing gum.

"All right," she said. "It's our little secret. Until you piss me off again."

"Of course," I said, mock serious, until she guffawed. She bobbed her body up and down at me like Jessica Rabbit. She grabbed the card when I tried to throw it away, shouting,

"No, this is a lifetime memento of your one true love. Oh, Nick! Sweet Nick!"

I shushed her and hid it while she laughed. Mr McGregor

stared at us over his rimless glasses as he padded by, carrying his manila folders.

I shuffled around her for the rest of the day. I blushed. I looked embarrassed. I made it look like I liked a boy and that she'd found me out. Rather than looking like 'the other'. I really do love your tits, Janine. Your bra strap has slipped down, let me help you. She winked at me as she got onto the number four after school, and my heart thudded like rain onto the bus stop roof. I saw her say something to Dan Aldridge as she sashayed to the back of the bus. He laughed and leered as he stood up to give her the window seat. She waved at me through the misty glass, like an ironic carnival queen. Exhaust fumes plumed in her wake.

By the time I got home, I was wistful and tired. I came up to my bedroom and slammed the door. I swung my school bag onto the bottom of the bed and my textbooks slid out into a haphazard fan. Blazer off, shoes off. I scrambled up the bed to lay my head on the pillow. Fairy lights and paper hearts glowed on the ceiling. The window was all misted up. I closed my eyes. Her auburn hair, the frizz halo around her face. Those pearl studs that belonged to her grandmother. Her ponytail, so keen and high. The pink lace of her bra. The light hair in the small of her back.

The door handle. I gasped.

"Phone for you."

My sister smirked at me and swung on the door knob.

I sat up. "Who is it?"

"Some guy called Nick. Janine told him to call, *apparently*. And Mum says, do you want tea?"

"Oh no," I groaned, dropping back onto my elbows. My sister wolf-whistled. I rolled my eyes. "But, yes, please, to tea."

ON THE BUS TO BICESTER

Gerlinde

yes! Our seats are still free

look

I think they're fighting   who?

our neighbours

WHAT A TRIFLE IS A HEART

Sarah Milne Das

There was a girl who, once upon her youth, she gave her heart away.

The girl exchanged her heart for nothing — that is what it is to gift — and for no regret, either — that is what it is to love.

Each day she gave her love a little more, a little more.

"I give you my heart," she whispered to his searching, kissing lips.

"I give you my heart," she called to him, each time they parted, each time reunited.

"I give you my heart," she sang to him as they danced as lovers, swirling together.

She gave him her laughter, her yearning, her smiles, the silken skeins of her wishes and dreams. This is what we mean, when we say the heart. The heart is all of this, and yet more —

The ease of spinning stories to our beloved when day ends, the catch of an eye that says I am understood and you are understood, the brush of a touch that says I know you are there, I know your contours well, and when we part, when we are apart, still bound with slender thread.

And her heart was her trust, and her heart was her hope, and her heart was her incautious joy that gave and gave and never feared.

And her heart was golden and beautiful, and fragile as spun sugar, but it lived and grew as long as she knew that she poured it into her love.

This boy who held her heart, perhaps he held it lightly. Perhaps he held it carelessly, left it on trains and park benches. The girl knew him to be absent-minded, but gradually, more often, she found him simply absent.

And as she had to tug him to her more and more and harder, the thread that bound them chafed, and she saw it fraying, unspooling. By her side he arrived at last, but something dear was missing —

"Where is my heart?" the girl cried.

He bowed his head like a nervous foal, and looked where she was not. "I cannot find it," he muttered, "I do not know — but it is no matter —"

"We will find it together," she promised, and she knelt beside him and stroked with soothing fingers.

She brushed down his sides and looked in his pockets, in the soles of his shoes and behind his ears. Flipped through his wallet and shook out his coat, but found only loose change and receipts. Not only the heart was lost, but the harmony they two had spun. He flinched from her touch, it tickled, annoyed; he went left, and she right; they fumbled.

"I shall grow it anew and give it again," she said, but it came out a question; she tried again — "I could give you more of my heart, that is, if you wanted…"

The boy shrugged.

She tried, she did, but the heart cannot grow strong if not caught by desire. The new fibres of heart grew twisted and brittle, snapped into splinters and cut the boy's hands. His fingers snatched back from the shards.

The boy backed away and away and away, out of her life and her story.

Still there was the girl, and she felt her heart shatter inside her.

Sharp fragments flew into her lungs, and tore with tiny stinging cuts until she gasped for breath and gurgled red.

Glassy splinters broke out through the skin of her back and breast, tearing all who came close, and digging deep when she tried to rest.

And with each movement the jagged remains of her heart scraped past each other, rasping out an ugly wail to haunt her every step.

"Make it stop," begged the girl of the wisest woman she knew. "Give me a cure, make me numb, take the pain away forever."

The wise woman shook her head gently; her voice was kind and tender.

"There is no cure but time and will, but that cure will come for you, I promise."

"I cannot wait," the girl moaned in pain. "I will find another way."

There is another way, and it is this. The girl removed her heart from her chest. Bit by tiny bit, piece by shattered piece, she plucked the fragments out and then she dropped them, bloody and hanging with flesh, into a bowl of bleach.

"No more pain," she whispered with each wince and each flinch, "This is the last of my pain, this and no more."

Hours she worked, picking delicately as a seamstress, teasing out each glimmer of heart embedded deep inside. She scraped carefully around the ribs for hidden splinters, lifted out each organ to search beneath for errant scraps.

Finally the bowl was full of darkened deadened remnants, and the girl felt lighter and emptier, with space to spare in her chest. All that was left where the heart once lived was the smallest golden root, beating oh so gently and glistening like sugar.

The girl lifted up her scalpel.

THE VIOLINIST

Tiffany Williams

He was a waiter. He had been there a few weeks, but the waiters all seemed to blend into one general young guy, and Vic avoided young guys in general. It was late on a Friday, the time of night most of the guests had had their pizzas and half-chickens with chips and moved on to make the most of the nightlife in Wolverhampton town centre. It was still quiet out there with the students away for the summer, and the atmosphere had carried over to the hotel.

She was at her station, grating parmesan and watching the plates go back and forth out of the corner of her eye, when a familiar high-pitched crash sang out across the kitchen. It was one of the tiny glass ketchup bowls the waiters always tried to balance on the edge of their hands.

"Job opening!" one of the other cooks called. She rolled her eyes at the crass joke and glanced over to the counter. The waiter was still standing there, frozen to the spot beside the countless pieces of broken glass, forcing a laugh.

It was like her friend Lizzy had always said. You got a radar for it after a while. She noticed it in the way he would walk around with his shoes untied for minutes at a time, but look around for a tissue the moment somebody sneezed. It was also there in the dark circles around his eyes, the lines at the corners of his lips and the slight puffiness in his cheeks. She had the same characteristics herself, but as they combined with her excessive height, her heavy dark hair which went from bob to birds' nest in a matter of hours, and the frown that had been her resting face since she was six months old, she was pretty sure she looked like a hag at twenty eight.

His face, however, was clear and bright. It was a thin face with a sharp nose and cheekbones, but any edge in him, literal or metaphorical, was blunted by the earnestness of his smile. His lips had a natural upward curve, and even when he was completely at rest, leaning against the doorway between the kitchen and the main dining room, she felt something she could only describe as *sunshine* coming from him.

Even so, he didn't fit in at Smestow Valley Hotel, at least not with the other waiting staff. She noticed he would always stand with them and nod along, but the conversation went straight through him. The real him was elsewhere.

Later that night, she was outside unlocking her bike to go home, when she heard him making a phone call she had made a hundred times.

"Thank you so much, I'm so sorry, it's just when these late shifts come up, I just have to...no, but, I told you I'd pick her up at nine and now I've taken up your whole evening...well, thanks. Was she alright? She is in bed, isn't she?"

She walked away, imagining she could send some telepathic message to him. *I get it. You're one of me, I'm one of you.*

Her first idea to get to know him better was to go to the waiting staff's little staff room and work out his name from the rota. It was Tobias Adler. *Almost as antique as Victoria Woodward*, she thought, *we have so much in common.*

This was also her last idea; she had never been good at

these things. What would she ever say to Lizzy? "I met a nice man. At least, I have been in the same room as him several times"? Not much, even by her standards. The chance happened by itself, one Saturday when the hotel was booked for a private party. She started late as she had to take Sam to Lizzy's, a decision she regretted when she saw a bouncy castle being inflated in the Barcelona Lounge.

"What are we making for the kids?" she asked the souschef, gloves on, ready to do whatever he suggested. She started every day determined to value his opinions.

"They can eat what their mums and dads eat."

This determination never lasted very long.

"They need something simpler. I've been bringing food home for Sam for years. He eats better than we do. But he still wouldn't eat bloody crab. I'm making cheese and ham sandwiches."

"You're on your own, then, Vicky."

She ground her teeth in frustration. When she made mistakes, nobody let her blag them off. And she knew who would be taking credit if the parents liked the kids' food. And they both knew who had been invited to apply for sous-chef first. And her name was *Vic*, not Vicky. Ranting to herself, she almost didn't see Tobias there, staring at the cutlery like he was waiting for it to tell him to lay it up. She leant across the counter and called out to him.

"Listen, er..." She realised she had better pretend not to know his name. "It's a bit of a hazard asking someone who's not qualified, but...do you know how to make a sandwich?"

As they worked, she found that he agreed with her about the crab.

"My daughter'd be traumatised. 'The Little Mermaid' is her favourite."

"My son loves looking at the crabs in the market. I tried to explain to him what they're there for, but I think he ignored me."

He was a father of one. His daughter was five and just starting school. They lived in a rented flat on the bottom floor of a house that was so old the door had shrunk in its frame and let a draught in, and the muck in the oven was probably older than both of them put together. But it was also the best they'd ever lived in so far. He'd been doing part-time restaurant work for years; it let him organise his life around her. Vic said it was the same for herself, in a way.

"I've wanted to do this since I was about ten. I had to cook for myself and my sister Tress while our dad was at work. She still lives with me now, so I can't have been that bad."

"Busy house," he remarked, sounding more impressed than empathetic.

"No, it's just three of us. My son's name is Sam, he's seven. Tress...Tress and I look after him together."

She waited for him to make a comment about this, maybe something awkward about which of them would teach him to wire a plug. He did not.

"Is it just you and Chloe?" she asked.

"Yes. My — her mum passed on when she was a baby."

Were you married to her? Vic wondered. *Were you together at all? Did you plan to have a baby together?* Whatever the story was, at least he had stuck around. They must have been young; seeing him up close, she thought he was maybe twenty eight like her, at most.

"I'm sorry," she said.

"Thank you. We get by alright."

A moment of calm working silence passed.

"How am I doing?" Tobias asked her.

She noticed he couldn't seem to cut the cheese to anything like the same thickness each time, but if the kids coming to this function were anything like Sam, they probably liked chunky sandwiches.

"They look great, thank you."

He'd been nervous. He released his grip on the tiny sandwich he was holding. His fingers had left tiny warm dents in the bread.

"We can't use that one," she said. She noticed she didn't sound like herself; she was smiling. "Eat it."

She looked back at the work and let the short time go by, become something good and precious. She wasn't going to ruin it by telling him about Sam's father.

They started walking back together, just for the ten minutes up to his bus stop. They swapped stories about the kids, about life, and some of them went on so long they had to swap numbers to finish by text.

```
And so now I have a pencil pot saying Happy
100 Birthday Mummy
Clo has been telling the kids at school
that we have a cat and its gonna have kittens
and now she's allowed to bring them to show.
its a toy im pretty sure its not pregnant.
```

Anyone watching them from the outside might have thought that Vic was looking for a father for Sam. It was the kind of romance that would happen at Christmas, and the following lack of it was the kind of disappointment that would weigh on a woman in January. But Sam had seen other kids' dads in his time and learned what they were about, and had still never asked for one of his own.

This, whatever it was, was about something else.

"The only time I've lived away from here is when I was training in Birmingham," she told him, one evening. "My college had a tradition with Le Chateau. The best students of every year got offered a job there over the summer, though they always had spaces for pot washers and such as well for anyone else. Everything has to be the best possible quality. You're trying to take people to heaven. But...because it's so hard, and so important, they teach you everything. So you can step up, you know. Every part of you goes into the fold, body and soul. Just being there....there's nothing like it in the whole world."

"So...were you one of the best students or a pot washer?" Tobias asked her.

It occurred to Vic that she hadn't exactly said. "One of the, er, good students. I was a bit obsessed! I was nineteen. Long time ago now."

"Tell me about it," he said with a soft smile. "That's when I had Chloe."

He was a violinist, though Vic was the one who used the word, after he explained that he'd played at pubs and open mic nights as soon he was old enough to drink.

"I only ever had one proper gig. It was at a pub on St Patrick's Day, they wanted Irish folk music. I'd usually done old composers at school, I had to practice like mad. I remember my dad said to me, is it worth it for thirty quid and a pint? It turned out it was."

"If you get paid, it's professional!"

"Cash in hand doesn't count. Anyway, I sold it before Chloe was born."

"Do you ever miss it?"

He thought. "I don't know. Most days I don't even think about it. There isn't much of that left in me now."

They came to a stop in the middle of the pavement. Vic felt something drawing her to hold his hand, but instead they just held eye contact and smiles.

"...Anyway," he said, again. "Let's hope they've behaved themselves tonight."

"...Yeah," was all Vic could say in response.

When she looked away she saw the first thing they always saw when they approached the corner where they'd separate, in big white letters, Fast Tan Salon. She'd gotten to know all the landmarks they passed, and she always hoped the time between them would somehow get longer.

She came home that evening to see the living room coffee table swamped in pizza boxes. A movie flashed on the TV. The three of them — Sam, Tress, and Louise, a girl Tress had met at uni — were bundled up on the sofa in a tangle of arms and legs.

Sam turned round to her and beamed. "Hi, Mum. Louise got us pizza."

"Aren't you a lucky boy, Pumpkin?"

She looked closer. Two large pizza boxes, a garlic bread box, and an empty bottle of Coke. On a Tuesday. How on earth were they going to settle him after this?

"How much -"

"Shhh..." Louise said. "This is my favourite bit."

"Right," she said, a little more abruptly than she really meant.

Tress turned, or rather rolled over as she was almost horizontal on Louise's lap.

"Leave off. He was upset," she said in a low whisper. "Those kids again."

Sam was big-boned. Vic reckoned it was ultimately down to nature; he'd be a big man when he grew up, like her dad. However, he'd also inherited his auntie's soft nature, and the bullies at school could smell him coming a mile off. Worst of all, he didn't have a big sister to defend him as Tress had had. Vic started to think through what she'd say the next time she met Sam's teachers. It was a battle that never seemed to end, for him most of all.

Her thoughts were interrupted by Sam laughing out so loudly he seemed to surprise even himself. Louise laughed in sync with him.

"Yes, yes, yes, YES! Get him!"

"This is why this is my favourite bit."

The tension went out of Vic at once. It was a school night and for once Sam was happy. Everything else could come just a bit later. She put her things aside and sat on the floor to the side of their little sofa. They'd been three alone for all these years and the house matched that; perhaps at the weekend they'd look at expanding.

The movie ended past Sam's bedtime, and as being a killjoy was one of Vic's natural talents, she volunteered to move him along and let Tress and Louise take some time for themselves. As she handed him his nightly mug of milk, she noticed he was watching her, his big hazel eyes serious.

"You OK, Pumpkin?" she asked him softly.

He sighed. "Mum, do you call me Pumpkin because I'm fat?"

"No," she said, kneeling on the floor so her face was level with his. "You're not fat. I call you Pumpkin because when you were born, you came out orange. The midwife said "Oh, this ain't right", but I said I'd love my orange baby with all my heart..."

"Mum!" Sam whined, collapsing dramatically on his bed, almost spilling his milk.

She got up and rescued his cup. "Alright, I'll tell you the truth. It was your first Halloween. And I'd said to Auntie Tress the whole time coming up to it that I couldn't be bothered doing anything for it. We were too tired, because you were still waking up in the night."

"I'm sorry," Sam murmured.

"Don't worry, Pumpkin, all babies are like that. Then on the morning of Halloween, I woke up and I had this great urge inside to dress you up and make you look cute. Cut*er*, I should say. So your auntie got one of your tops, which was orange, and drew lines and a face on it with felt tip. Then we found a green tea-towel and made it into a little hat, for your leaves. That night, you fell asleep with your pumpkin top on, and we decided since we'd put it on quite late, we wouldn't wake you up to change you. And that was the first time you slept all the way through the night. The night the ghosts come out, as well!"

Sam shrugged, the trace of a smile on his lips. "I ain't 'fraid of no ghosts."

"So from then on, you were Pumpkin. After the night you were so brave. And you haven't stopped being brave, even now."

She noticed that his eyes were at last starting to close for longer and longer, and she tucked him in once he got into bed.

"Goodnight, Mum," he whispered.

"Goodnight, Pumpkin."

Vic went to her room after this rather than downstairs to Tress and Louise. That was the first time in a while that she and Sam had had a story together before bed. It wouldn't be long until it stopped altogether. She took out her phone, suddenly inspired to text Tobias and tell him to treasure the time he had with Chloe, and it hit her very powerfully that she was thinking of him so easily, all the time, like he'd always been there.

She struggled to sleep that night, going over their conversations in her head. When she listened carefully she could hear her heart beating furiously, furtively, as if it didn't want the rest of her to notice. Understanding was something she'd given up expecting from men. She didn't know if she was in love, or afraid.

One night in February, just before Valentine's Day, Tobias told Vic out of the blue that he was taking a break over half-term, not only from work but also from parenting. Chloe was staying with family. It was sudden, and it panicked her.

`It'll be weird not seeing you,` his last text said.

`I do exist outside the hotel,` she replied. `Let's go for a drink.`

After a few minutes, he replied with, `I'd like that x`

With that 'x', the oxygen went out of her lungs. She barely took a breath as she confirmed it. Thursday, 7pm, Wetherspoons.

"Where is my lipstick?" Vic asked Tress.

"Sam ate it, remember?"

She groaned. "He's too old to be doing that kind of thing."

"He was three at the time."

"Oh."

Tress, luckily, had only recently started playing the make-up game herself, and offered her a bright red thing called 'Cannibal'. The first time she put it on, her mouth looked like one out of Sam's nursery paintings and she had to clean it off with some bunched-up toilet tissue. Make-up always went wrong when you needed it most.

She got a sudden flashback of the day she first met Mark's parents, at a garden party they were throwing. She had spent the whole morning making them a gateau, only getting herself ready at the last minute.

"Mmm," he'd murmured when she showed him the cake. "The thing is, Mum and Dad will already have plenty of food."

All the way there, she had stared at her face in his wing mirror, thinking she should have worked on that all morning instead. Once, at Le Chateau, Chef had compared her cooking to his wife's fungal nail. Somehow that still hadn't hurt like one of Mark's *Mmm*'s.

Alright, she said to herself, *you're thinking about him. Think about him for one minute, then stop.*

She thought of the last few months with him, just after Tress left for university. She'd relied on her job to fill as much of the day as possible, as every time she came home to find the house empty, she couldn't think straight until Mark was there.

And when he did come back he'd say "I'm tired, Vic, let's just go to bed."

When they first met he was the kindest man she had ever known. Whenever she got upset, about her parents or work or anything else, he would stroke her arms and tell her he was so proud of her. And then, one day, he wasn't. The eight years that had passed since their split had taught her to cut herself a bit of slack; she'd had no friends, she'd lost her parents, the least she'd deserved was some kindness from the man she was closest to. But she still felt a twinge of mortification as she remembered following him up the stairs, putting his words aside, too keen to have a moment of his time, his *attention*.

With that in mind, it shouldn't have been such a shock when he finally admitted that he didn't love her any more.

She remembered the sound of his car, formerly known as the car, driving away for the last time. She remembered going straight to bed and covering herself with clothes and blankets until it felt like nothing could come through. She remembered the relentless dreams she had of him coming back, and how she could tell they were dreams because she always looked very pretty in them.

She remembered asking Tress — in a text, because she was too terrified to say it aloud — if it was normal for stress after a breakup to make you tired, hungry and miss your period.

"I would say *probably*," Tress had responded, but came straight home that weekend.

It was also Tress who volunteered to be the first to look at the pregnancy test. The first thing she said when she emerged from the bathroom was "I love you. Everything's going to be fine". To show she meant it, she dropped out of her course, and didn't go back for another two years.

A lot must have gone through her little sister's mind at that time. Vic didn't ask her about it too often. The point was that she had chosen to stay, and she was not going to leave them.

Vic finished her train of thought with those vanilla-scented days in the house before Sam was born. She had made a lot more cakes than Tress was able or willing to eat, but each one was a symbol of a good day. And now they really were very happy, and everything was going to be fine.

So why was she changing things?

"Have fun," Tress said, squeezing her tightly. "Don't do anything I wouldn't do."

"Where are you going?" Sam asked, with a mouth full of pasta.

"Shoe shopping," she said.

"Boring," he said, and looked back at his magazine.

It was raining so persistently outside that she had to hold her hands up to her face to protect her make-up. As she paced to the bus stop she stepped into a puddle, and felt the water instantly fill up the flimsy new shoes she'd bought from Shoe-Zone.

The buses were slow at this time of night. The people huddled under the shelter had the look of people who had been out all day, with heavyset expressions and bags of groceries cutting into their hands. She leaned against the shelter doorway and read and re-read a poster advertising a new type of Weetabix.

What was a first date supposed to feel like? She had to ask the question directly, as she did not trust herself to supply an honest answer without hard interrogation. Good, was what. Maybe not totally good, but somewhat good. What she felt was not good. She felt the wind through her coat and against her legs, and her shoes felt like they might start rotting. When she looked out towards the estate she could see the warm lights of windows, so familiar she'd never thought before of how nice they were. She checked her phone, hoping he might say he was stuck in traffic, or that he'd suddenly won the lottery and was moving to Barbados. He had not texted.

It'll be over by nine thirty, she said to herself. Two and a half hours, it's not a long time. Not even that late. When it's done, you can relax. Until you have to do it again, of course.

There was no reason that they wouldn't talk about the things they always talked about; Sam, Chloe, work, food, music, the football. But when she tried to sound the words of the conversation in her head, she found she couldn't.

She closed her eyes and tried a different tactic, picturing the pub instead. She had been there before with Lizzy, for Mums' Nights Out. They'd sit at those shiny wooden tables, Lizzy in a dress, Vic in her favourite jeans and trainers, and have double burgers and overfilled glasses of White Zinfandel. The pub was a converted old courthouse, and still had a fire, which they lit most evenings at this time of year. A kind, safe place, a place to let time go by. She had devoted her career to these kinds of places. When she tried to picture drinking with Tobias there, talking with him there, the images she conjured melted into something as empty and unwelcoming as this horrible night.

Less than five minutes until the bus arrived. She couldn't think at all. *She needed to, needed to...*

She needed change, for the bus. Without stopping to check her purse again, she made her way across the road to the cash machine outside the newsagents. It was one that charged for withdrawals but she would think about that in the morning.

When she turned around, the bus was leaving. It was so bright it seemed to emphasise rather than penetrate the dark.

She walked slowly back to the bus stop and glanced up at the little display that showed the times. The next one was in forty minutes. It was done. She had officially skipped her date. Her heart felt weird and unstable, like it had been moved slightly out of place.

It was one thing to be frightened of something upsetting. It was another thing to be frightened of something harmless. And it was a special and stupid thing to be frightened of something good. Nobody would understand, not even Tress, who understood almost everything. She would have to wait it out here. She was suddenly so exhausted it seemed easy.

At five minutes past seven, he texted I'm here.

At ten minutes past seven, he texted `The White Hart, right?`

At half past seven, he texted, `Please tell me I haven't got the wrong day lol`

At twenty to eight, he started calling. She stared at the phone and counted every ring, as if it made what she was doing less terrible. He called every eight or nine minutes; he was probably trying to hold on for ten. She remembered doing the same from a hundred other occasions. By half past eight, they stopped.

THE THREE MOST IMPORTANT WORDS

Elaine Roberts

Jason awoke on Saturday morning to a creeping hangover and Jessie's fingers tracing absent-minded patterns across his back. When past lovers had done this, it was as though their fingertips were leaving a trail of tingling fire against his skin. Jessie's touch left him completely cold. He lay perfectly still, hoping that she would not realise he had woken, and tried to drift back towards the pleasant dream in which he was fixing up his Honda. Unfortunately, a change in his breathing must have given him away, for she was soon draping herself across his body and pulling at his shoulders with her usual *you're up, Jason, good morning baby!*

"Yep. Hi," he mumbled thickly, and turned to give her a brief kiss on the lips. She rolled away from him and stretched, arching her back lasciviously towards the ceiling.

Jason screwed his eyes shut and pressed the heels of his palms into the sockets. They'd had booze delivered the night before, a riotous party had ensued, and now his mouth was dry and a thousand tiny jackhammers worked away at his skull. He sat up and threw the covers aside. The bedroom smelt of feet and desperation.

"Last night was fun, wasn't it?" Jessie had approached the mirror in her slip and was giving every appearance of checking her pores. But her eyes were fixed firmly on his reflection.

"Yeah."

"I've never laughed so much, have you?"

"Yeah. Er — no." He dug through his pile of clothes, jumbled precariously on a chair.

"I'm having *such* a great time with you, Jason," she said earnestly as she continued to watch him in the mirror. "And I just wanted to tell you again — "

Oh no.

"I just wanted to tell you again, baby, that I — "

Oh NO.

" — love you."

For God's sake.

There was a silence as Jason pulled on his jeans without looking at her, but he could see her anxious outline in his peripheral vision, waiting for a reply.

"Can we, er, can we not do this now, Jessie? Sorry." He found a clean T-shirt and tugged it over his head, then began to look around for his hair gel.

"You've said that already. I've told you how I feel, and all I need is — "

"I know what you need," snapped Jason. Yes, he could say the winning words any time he wanted, but he'd had the thudding realisation weeks ago that such a barefaced lie wouldn't be worth his pride. Still avoiding Jessie's eye, he wrenched open the bedroom door and strode towards the much more inviting smell of cooked breakfast.

She pattered after him into the kitchen, hissing, "You should say it back *today*, otherwise — oh!"

They stopped short at the sight of their housemates Liam and Zara in a tight embrace, she perched on the dinner table with her legs wrapped around his waist, he with his usual backwards baseball cap and bare chest, hands wandering all over the place, and their two sets of lips welded together as though there were no tomorrow. Their own sugary *I love yous* had been exchanged a solid month ago.

"Um — " Jessie said, by way of greeting.

"Sor-ee!" trilled Zara, pulling away from Liam, though her hands remained on his chest. "Liam cooked me breakfast, so I was just saying thank you!" A plate of sausages, scrambled eggs and baked beans lay dangerously close to her thigh. The beans, Jason noticed, had been arranged in a heart shape around the rim of the plate.

Jessie immediately turned to Jason. "Cook me breakfast too?"

The only frying pan in the house was slick with sausage grease, and Jessie was a vegetarian. Jason tossed the washing up bowl into the sink, set the water running and began to look for a fresh dishcloth.

"Thanks babe," Jessie said, then, "Love you," more quietly. Jason pushed the taps back as far as they would go; the water thudded even more noisily into the bowl.

Meanwhile, Zara had slid into her seat and was consuming her sausages slowly, and with a huge amount of concentration. While she ate, Liam dropped to his front and started doing those push-ups with a clap in between them, the kind that made Jason feel totally inadequate. After a sharp look from Jessie, Jason reluctantly abandoned the frying pan and sank into several push ups too, albeit the pedestrian, non-clap version. Both women kept their doe-eyed gazes on their partners, only breaking off to spare each other a brief disdainful glance.

It was the hottest day of the year so far; the four of them found some beach towels and spent several long hours lounging around in the garden. Jason pushed his sunglasses as far towards his face as they would go and pretended to be dozing whenever Jessie spoke to him.

At lunchtime, he slipped away to sit on the edge of their bed, where he clutched a fussy little hand mirror of Jessie's. He checked his chin stubble, then brought the mirror so close to his face that all he could see were his eyes. *There's me. The real, authentic me.* He even started fiercely muttering, "Integrity. True to myself. Proper authentic," over and over again, until Jessie sidled into the bedroom to ask who he was talking to, which culminated in another painful argument.

After that, neither couple spoke much, preferring to sunbathe in silence. At one point Jason turned to Liam, who, it turned out, he had bonded with the most, and said, "You decided to stay in as well today then, mate?"

Liam and Zara roared with laughter; their mirth made Jason forget his hangover for a few glorious moments.

They all went to speak to the Landlord one by one as the sun set. Jessie returned with red-rimmed eyes and pointed glances, and Jason tried not to imagine what she had said about him as he pushed his dinner morosely around his plate that evening.

What was he still doing here? Oh, it had been a right laugh in the first week, and his heart had even leapt with joy when he clapped eyes on the pretty girl he'd been paired with. But his euphoria was soon replaced with week after week of avoiding her doleful stares and tearful whines of *I wish you'd say it back*. Week after week of heart-judderingly awkward moments and embarrassed gapes from their peers. He could just walk away, but he wasn't a quitter, dammit — and what would the lads think of him if he abandoned such a great 'opportunity'? *The boys' advice would be invaluable at this point...* For what felt like the millionth time, his fingers twitched towards a smartphone that was not there.

At nine o'clock they gathered in the living room, Jessie sitting stiffly by his side, Liam and Zara stretched out on the sofa opposite, talking softly. And as the familiar, disembodied female voice hollered through the speakers, Jason's headache returned with a vengeance.

"Loveshack housemates, this is your host speaking!"

It'll all be over soon; I'll be a runner-up, and I may still have a shred of dignity intact.

"You are live on Channel 87, so please do not swear."

I can save those three words for the person I actually do love. And we'll be nowhere near Channel 87.

"For eight weeks we've watched the love stories, larks, and laments of ten FANTASTIC couples. Huge congratulations on being the final two pairs!"

I can get back to fixing up the Honda, see the lads at the pub every Friday. Normality.

"But who will the public vote as their winners?"

Best to stay single for a while too. Can't deal with any more nonsense like this.

"Will it be Jason and Jessie," — there was a wave of cheers from outside, and a few faint boos — "Or will it be Liam and Zara?" A tsunami of screams, whoops, 'awwws', cheers and stamping. Jessie's face seemed to crumple in on itself; Liam and Zara giggled complacently, eyes already shining in triumph, legs intertwined on their sofa.

The host spoke on.

"But wait! There's a final surprise, ladies and gentlemen! We've added a new prize, *on top of* the twenty thousand pounds cash and the exclusive *Hello!* photoshoot! Yes... the winning couple will enjoy joint ownership of a brand new, limited edition, top-of-the-range BMW M240 CONVERTIBLE!"

Oh.

Jason's head snapped up as the crowd went wild; Liam was looking at him shrewdly.

"The numbers are on your screens now! Lines close at 9.45, and I'll announce the winners at 10. Sit tight, Loveshack housemates… I'LL BE BACK SOON!"

Jason bided his time. Jessie was curled up miserably next to him, still holding his hand, but her fingers were limp and her shoulders hunched in defeat. At half past nine, he rose abruptly and pulled her towards the bedroom, ignoring Liam and Zara's suspicious gazes. Shutting the door, he positioned the bemused Jessie right in front of a camera, which whirred and clicked as it swivelled slowly around to face them.

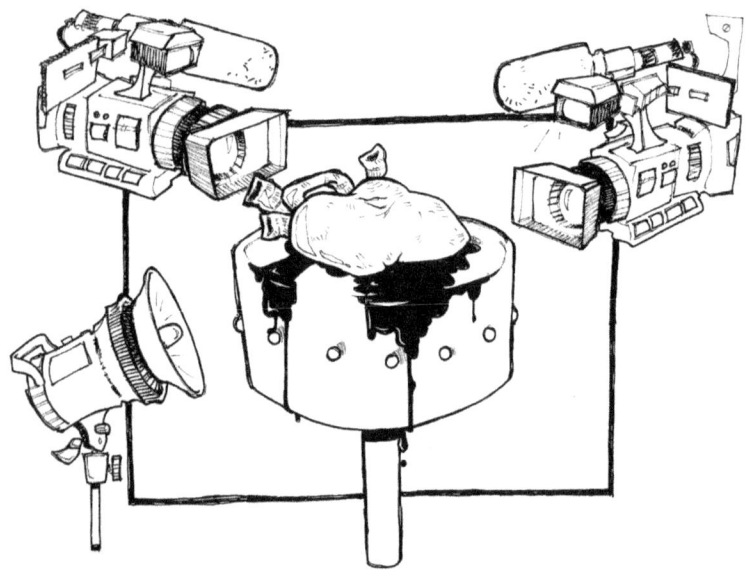

They've been voting for weeks to hear this… Well, bingo.

"Babe," he whispered urgently, "Babe, I've been thinking… I've got something to tell you…" He lifted a trembling hand and tucked a stray strand of hair behind her ear as they locked eyes. Her irises were hazel, flecked with blue, he noticed for the first time. The camera lens was firmly trained on his face.

He could already see *#jasonlovesjessie* rising to the top of the trending topics. The leather on those car seats was within sniffing distance. "I can't deny it any more, Jessie, I…"

GO WHEN THE LIGHT TURNS RED

Kevin Elliott

"You're comfortable?" George's voice echoed off the examination room's walls. Did the echo make him sound medical? He should learn what the equipment clustered around the walls did — one screen flickered into life as he spoke.

"As comfy as I get." Pete's voice bristled with pain, his legs twisted as he tried to keep them flat. "On Earth this chair would slice your buttocks open."

"Ah, it's not designed for Earth gravity. Are you ready?"

Pete nodded. "So to be certain, this isn't a cure."

"It might lead to a cure — we can't tell. Just keep still. The sensors will cope with most movements, but don't kick."

"No ballet then?"

"No Pete, not today."

George swivelled his chair to face Pete and flicked at the slate on his lap. Pete's body always did its own thing — a puppet under nobody's control — but now thin bands of gold light wrapped Pete's limbs and twitched as he twitched. A ghost-like copy of Pete appeared beside him and copied his posture, transparent limbs synchronised with the real ones.

"I'll add in the pain display."

Pale blue and red patches burst onto the ghost's surface, growing and fading each second.

"Can you see those?" said George.

Pete's gaze darted over the image. He lolled back and the red swathes grew until they merged and sheathed his lower torso. "Yes, you've got it."

"Muscular pain in red, skeletal in blue. Anything cardiac will appear in purple, renal is yellow. Try moving from one side to the other."

"Ooh, buttock shuffling, my favourite." Pete heaved his body to his left. The red wash shunted lower down and shaded into brilliant crimson around the base of the ghost's spine.

"Yes, my back's screaming now." Pete shifted back, sweat beaded his face. "It's beautiful, George, artists will weep. Doctors will see what hurts and diagnosis will speed up." Pete paused. "But data needs interpreting — you'll still need a human."

"They'll have data." George brandished his slate at Pete. "We record every twinge and our pattern-spotting software reduces diagnosis times. Doctors spend time with you and not your symptoms."

"Good stuff, but seeing pain isn't experiencing pain." Pete winced and fell silent for a few seconds. "Colours only outline the general pain type, doctors won't know the effect it has, how it affects your breathing or your eyesight or your heartbeat. You're turning pain into data, but can you run things the other way, let a doctor experience pain in real time? Pain teaches more than images."

"It's possible," George's voice softened. "Pain to data, data to pain. But you'd want a second machine and a second machine…"

"Costs money. We've been on the same pay grade for three years — and this looks like an expensive hobby."

"My savings built that interface box. We can store data and run it back to the first interface, but turning data into pain means re-configuring everything: two days' work. Two days for each patient."

"So real time diagnosis needs a second machine," said Pete. "Any thoughts?"

Pete grimaced and his ghost clothed itself in dark red; his pain made the decision easy.

"Loans might be possible; there's someone I should contact," George said.

George stared at the floor as Steph walked in; Pete stared. Today an immaculate suit fitted her curves. Steph was proud of her size; she had to buy bespoke suits but George suspected she'd become a lawyer so money wouldn't be a problem. Trousers, jacket, everything in dark blue wool; she'd chosen wool because sheep couldn't live on the moon, and there was enough wool here to fit two average women.

Steph had confidence for three. She sat beside the steel grey cabinet of his second interface machine — delicate equipment he'd assembled by mortgaging his life.

"What am I seeing here?" Steph's voice was its usual cocktail of assurance and smoothness.

"This is Pete, our test subject." Pete nodded back, perching on the reclining chair, legs twitching.

"Good to see you, Pete." Steph broke into a smile. "I heard George was looking for people with Scott's."

Pete grinned. "For once I'm a good example."

"You said this wasn't a cure," Steph said.

"Not for Scott's, no." George checked his slate. "Scott's is hard to treat, but this helps doctors know what hurts, how pain spreads when the patient moves, how breathing changes when muscular pain kicks in."

"Pain has flavours," Pete said. "They're difficult to describe. I've got words, but other people with Scott's use different words for the same pain. We don't understand what another person feels at any moment, so we can't agree names for the flavours and doctors end up confused. This machine gives us vocabulary, one colour for each flavour. Say you're feeling blue and doctors will understand. Shifting puts pressure on my spine. Usually I avoid pain, but glance to your right…"

Steph studied Pete's ghost and blue rings sheathed the ghost's spine.

"It hurts, but you can see it hurts." Pete closed his eyes.

"You developed this, George?" asked Steph.

"I set up the neural interface. It's not bulky, our receptors follow most movements."

"Impressive." Steph sat beside George and crossed her legs.

"The interface works both ways. We can turn colours back into sensations, even pain." said George. "There's a thousand people with Scott's syndrome on the moon and not enough doctors; this should speed up diagnosis."

George watched as Steph leant back and arched her arms behind her head. "I don't like to inflict pain on you, Steph, but a demonstration would let you experience Pete's sensations."

"Oh, pain has a place in every relationship; two of my novels make that point." Steph blinked twice, a smile played around her lips. Had her voice deepened?

"I've set this up for you." George tapped his slate and gold bands spiralled around Steph's frame. "This will hurt, but…"

"So long as the pain is tasteful," Steph said. "There may be a story here, though I don't focus on extremes…Arghhh, my legs, what are you doing?" Steph lurched to her left, almost falling from her chair.

"That's what Pete feels each day."

"Turn it off, I can't…turn it off…" Her cheeks glowed an angry red, her mouth twisted into a grimace.

"That's mild; maybe three out of ten," Pete said. "Turn it

down, George."

"It's not calibrated for others yet. People perceive pain differently, so give me a second." George's fingers stroked his slate. "Better?"

Steph sat up, her face flushed. "Dear God, is that what you feel Pete? All the time?"

"We have to guess at the intensity, but that's what my spine says. If I lean forward…"

A reddish-brown stain crept over the ghost's lower body, cloaking the translucent bones inside. Steph writhed and a shuddering hiss escaped her lips.

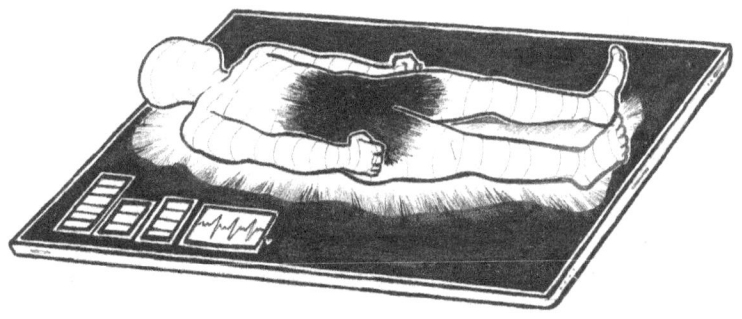

"That's muscular pain," Pete said. "The moon recycles everything: water, food, air, now agony."

Steph closed her eyes and exhaled. "This is brilliant work, George; it'll speed up diagnosis. But."

"There's a but?"

"There's an issue." Steph swept her hand through her hair and checked her blouse. "I remember a twenty-year-old case. Three doctors tested a new anti-radiation drug on themselves, but they rushed everything and didn't plan. After their test this base was down three doctors."

"I'd not heard," George said.

"Perils of being a lawyer, your bedtime reading is gruesome. Government slammed legislation into place; now doctors can't test on themselves and it's illegal to help doctors test on themselves. Wire a doctor to this machine and you'll face a savage jail sentence."

"This isn't real pain — we're sharing, not testing."

"You can make a case but the law will see it differently. You might find a sympathetic judge, but they only have so much freedom to interpret cases. I'm sorry, George, I know what this means to you, but medical safety isn't the same as legal safety. Other lawyers will give you the same story. I could talk with my pet politician about amending the law, but that's expensive."

George stayed silent as his mind totted up the money he'd spent, the hours he'd spent applying for loans, his future bundled into the steel cabinet beside Steph. He'd vacuumed his saving account clean and in two weeks they'd ask for the first loan payment. He imagined red numbers crawling over a screen — if he slept tonight their minus signs would come snapping for him.

"Are you all right, George?" she asked. Steph's voice became a seductive burble, nudging his ear.

"Apart from being buried under the debt mountain, apart from having two diagnosis machines I can't use, apart from having wasted six months on..."

"Sometimes you need to think sideways." Steph stood up and smoothed her trousers. "I have two jobs. My main job is the law; it tells me what's legal. My other job shows me what's possible."

"Your other job, writing those steamy thrillers?"

"Erotica, George, I don't do steam. Pete, could you stay hooked to this wonderful device for a few minutes and do some reading?"

"One of your naughty books?"

"Yes, one of my naughty books. No need to read out loud, but if George links us I'll sense your reactions.

"I'm due at work now." George had laboured through the night; today's work would make a revolting stew, regret churned with a fight against sleep. He should have spoken to Steph earlier.

"We'll chat later," she said. "I should spend time with Pete. A little literary criticism for the early morning, courtesy of radio George."

Tiredness doused his anger. George stood in his clammy clothes, creased reminders of the hours he'd spent chasing this dream.

"Anything to help you, Steph." George forced the words out. "I'll hook you together, and Pete will tell you when he's had enough." He remade the link and gold bands played over Steph's limbs to mirror those reforming around Pete.

He couldn't afford coffee now; soon he might not afford air.

Steph slid her slate from an elegant black leather handbag and handed it to Pete. "Here's a story set in Victorian England."

"All steam trains and horses?"

"Normally I ask people what they think, but George's machine should show me your opinion."

Pete balanced the slate on his arm, his fingers curled to grip and stroke the

glowing surface. His eyes flickered over the screen. Some men would only read her writing in private, but Pete's physical problems meant he could ignore other people's opinions.

Steph waited. Pete's pain remained, a nagging sensation, an aggressive cousin of pins and needles bunched around her lower spine. She'd stick with it. George had set his machine to filter out agony and Steph was more interested in Pete's reaction — especially his non-verbal reaction.

"And that's why they're called bodice-rippers," said Pete.

"What about the next section?"

Pete's mouth hung open, and a fluttering sensation wriggled over Steph's chest, her throat became dry, her breath quickened as golden light slid over her chest and head. How had George translated the feelings? How had he crossed the gender divide — turning Pete's arousal into her arousal? What had made him thorough enough to rig the interface to handle both pleasure and pain? He'd done a superb job, and her writing wasn't bad either.

Steph gasped and Pete stopped reading. "You want me to carry on?"

She fought to keep her voice level, but sensation ebbed away from her, like a dream after waking. "Keep reading, there's a good bit coming."

"It's well written, I can picture the people involved. Must be funny doing that under Earth gravity, you'd think the man's legs would break, but..."

"Keep reading."

Pete smirked, but returned to the scene. Again she sensed the stoking and arousal, so different from her past encounters. These implanted sensations had a robust quality, a flavour of haste and urgency like a force hustling her towards a cliff edge. Steph settled back, letting breath sigh from her open mouth as bands of light swooped around her head and chest.

"You're distracting me, Steph."

"I know where you've reached," she said. "And George has good news."

"So there we are." Steph settled back into her leather chair. Not a luxury, an investment, a vital component in the image she gave her clients. Even George. "Three weeks ago we only had your prototype. Now there's proof of concept, a patent application and a business plan. I've established an excellent credit line so there's cash to refine the interface and I've found a manufacturer. Production starts next month."

"Are there any blocking issues?" asked George, sniffing at his coffee.

"Paying for air makes me cautious, and as I've invested a fair chunk of my savings in your work, I checked everything. Politically things may become sensitive, but I sounded out a few senators and we shouldn't face serious opposition. Once we have enough cash we'll lobby for a change in the law. I'll leave technical details to you, but you should leave your day job, this venture will make more each day than you do in a month. Build a team."

"Can we employ Pete? He wants to work."

"Sure. Having someone cheeky on board will keep us careful, and the money this brings in will buy him decent care. We're helping couples with their sex lives, we make money by producing new forms of erotica, and..."

"I'll never show my face at an engineering conference again. Never thought I'd be working in the porn industry; it's..."

"George! How many times? This is erotica, not porn."

"Erotica and porn, right. Two words with one meaning."

"Imagination versus physics, George, there's the difference. We're helping people with Scott's and other conditions. It's all about finding the right question — we started off asking how we could help people in pain."

"And now?"

"Pain is just one experience — selling experiences gives us power to help people. Tap into primal urges and everything becomes possible."

LEAVE, LEAVE FAIRE BRIDE, YOUR SOLITARY BED

'Doc' David

She couldn't get it out of her head. The fragility. The sadness. She never recovered from it, realising this only now. It took a lonely hotel room, and the traffic sounds on London's Euston Road, for her to finally come to terms with the fact. The sobbing was her own. She rocked softly on the bed, knees up beneath her chin, and when she glanced at the mirror by the door she threw a shoe at it. The figure in the mirror, looking back at her in a party frock , clutching a pillow, was a pathetic specimen.

Cast your mind back to that ridiculous skirt, what they called an ankle-sweeper in its day, with its bold as brass heavy wool pattern of swirling leaves. For many years that's all she remembered of the incident — that skirt, those leaves — as if her brain had blanked out a trauma to leave a flighty detail in its place, gnawing away in perpetuity. A paisley pattern instead of the grand alternative.

To say the incident had been odd would be an understatement, but she was young back then and such a thing didn't bother her the way it evidently does now. So very few things bothered her in 1980 that she had quite the reputation among her friends and peers. She was the "fifteen-minute girl", because more than once she had arrived for class only in time to see it draw to a close. The lecturers at her college in Oxford described it as lamentable, taking Sandra aside to ask whether she felt it worthwhile to invest any more effort — not just her's but everybody's — in pursuing a career in book keeping.

"Ms Setters," they said, "you have a come-day, go-day attitude."

So true. She had a "come-day, go-day attitude", although she didn't care to admit it. So she bowed her head in the common room, reverentially toward the members of staff, as if to say she had no idea and would endeavour to try harder from now on. It wasn't entirely her fault. "Swear down," she said in her defence in that accent that was hard to ignore, "my mam's been poorly."

Sandra remained a student rascal. She did not like book keeping. She didn't like that sort of discipline because there was nothing romantic about it, no room for flexing the creative muscle. She wanted to study the metaphysical poets, not mathematical formulae, but was informed on open day that she wouldn't get anywhere with an accent like that. It was a boy who said it, pretty comfortable in his boating shoes. She on the other hand was miles from home and awkward. She gave him a mischievous tap with her elbow. "That would be funny if it wasn't so true," she told him.

So Sandra did not go to Merton. She was not pursuing the words of Andrew Marvell and John Donne and all of those poets, as she so wanted, surrounded by Medieval trappings, but in one of the other colleges, pursuant of sums instead.

Which is why it was so refreshing to meet Mr Baker. He too had a reputation, albeit a very different one to hers. He was going nowhere fast, saying so himself, but then he was old and bits were starting to fall off anyway. "Don't get old," he once advised Sandra.

Now in a hotel room on the Euston Road, the woman in the mirror realises, perhaps too late, that she had gotten old. Sandra rocked gently and sobbed on the bed, her mascara tunnelling through the orbits of her eyes toward unfathomable pits of despair. There was one week to go before her wedding day and suddenly all she could think about was Mr Baker and that strange business of thirty years ago.

Merton College 1980.

It was dark and the snow glistened in the light from the windows. The Christmas carol service started late that midweek evening because Mr Baker, the stand-in church organist, had insisted on telling another one of his stories. It was outside the Chapel of St Mary and St John, beside the Christmas tree in the Front Quad that he cornered more hapless passers-by, first-year students in this instance. He had visited the cheapest bar in Oxford and because of it, because of the several nip bottles of particularly strong ale, the story he was telling was not likely to end soon. Mr Baker and the students, too polite to turn away, were covered in the snow that was falling again.

This was the Sandra's first impression.

Sandra had been inside the chapel waiting for the carol service to start, not knowing then the cause of the hold up.

It was bitterly cold in the chapel, but attendance was high. The service was a popular one and reservations had to be made well in advance. The congregation comprised mainly of students, many of them from Merton, who arrived straight from dinner in the Hall in their smart clothes. Some, like Sandra, were from one of the other colleges. Still, Sandra did not expect to be sitting alone. As everyone filed in, the Chaplain ticked names from a list. She was escorted to a seat that happened to be away from everyone she knew. It was close to the magnificent chapel organ, and, unfortunately, closer to the door too. She plucked from the bench a notice of reservation on which her name was misspelled. (Not enough S's.)

"Oh," she said, and plonked herself down.

The bench was uncomfortable and the blood rapidly drained from Sandra's buttocks. Making matters worse was the family with restless children seated to her left, while on her right was a shaggy individual with a pokey manner. He was controlling the sound and lights of the chapel, his fingers wrapped round a little control unit with knobs on that looked like it was from the 1950s. He smiled at Sandra.

Sandra fidgeted. She pulled her hands from her coat pockets to blow into her hands to try to warm them, and she danced her toes inside her shoes. She threw glances at her friends seated far away in the ante-chapel, leaning forward in her seat to get a better look and then throwing herself back again to the chagrin of all those around her.

"The fifteen-minutes girl," someone nearby said in a poor facsimile of her own accent.

It was too much. She decided with a grunt that the long wait was unacceptable, and if she did not act now her bones may never recover from the bitter cold. Sandra got up to leave, in spite of the bells of the chapel ringing out, suggesting that things were happening at last. The choir was itching to get started. She passed them as a chorister was stepping forward, his mouth anticipating the first vowel of an old German carol with a large O shape. The sound seemed to come from Heaven itself. But Sandra was committed now. She had to leave.

Before her the dark November evening was lapping at the open door, and then appeared the vicar in an anxious state. He was in and out of the door, checking his wristwatch and tutting because Mr Baker, the stand-in organist, was nowhere to be seen.

It was a surprise to see the vicar run passed her like that.

She had reached the oak door of the Hall, which was cast in light from the Library, all the more ethereal because of the distant song of the chorister. The sound of snow crunching underfoot made her turn. For one dizzy moment Sandra thought the vicar was coming for her, at her, that he might grab her and take her back to the carol service. She instinctively skipped aside, whereupon she lost her footing and fell down with an "oomph".

The vicar stopped to help Sandra to her feet. He was most apologetic. He told her he was looking for Mr Baker, as if that explained everything. Then he pointed to the Front Quad.

"Mr Baker," he said.

The man with the small audience by the Christmas tree was as old as the college walls, with quite the reputation. He liked his drink for one thing, and his dress was ill advised. Even on a bleak evening such as this one, deep in snow, he wore only sandals on his feet and no socks. A thin jacket and trousers covered his gaunt frame, while on his head was something that belonged in the sun, a brightly coloured prayer towel of Indian origin. He leaned on a walking stick. The two students, to whom he was talking, were far less enamoured than he to be out in the cold. The cold appeared to have no adverse effect on him, and he delivered his story as if he had all the time in the world — as if November at Merton College was another lazy afternoon on the banks of the Ganges, one and the same, flowing here from its source of Gaumukh.

Mr Baker might still be telling that story had the vicar not been looking for him.

The vicar did not venture out from the arch of the Hall. He favoured sanctuary from the falling snow, his hands plunged deep in his cassock, frightened to get his cassock wet. Instead he made noises from beneath the arch to attract Mr Baker's attention.

Sandra Setters tread carefully round him, lest she slip and fall again. Her arms wobbled by her sides, like a pole in a high wire act. She continued gingerly across the quad, ostensibly toward the exit. But on reaching Mr Baker, the centre of everyone's attention, she stopped.

He was talking to the students about an arcane ritual that takes place once a year at the college. If they knew what he was talking about they didn't show it. In the autumn, members of the college, in full academic dress, mark the change from British Summer Time to Greenwich Mean Time. As he was divulging this information, the vicar over by the arch was calling his name.

"Hoo hoo, Mr Baker! Mr Baker!"

Mr Baker seemed not to notice. He turned to Sandra.

"Hello, my dear," Mr Baker said by way of introduction. "The Merton Time Ceremony. Are you familiar with it?"

Sandra shook her head.

"Hoo hoo, Mr Baker! Mr Baker!"

"Well, let me tell you. Once a year, in the autumn, an arcane ritual takes place that is called the Merton Time Ceremony. It's closed to members of the public, and indeed anyone who is not a fully-fledged member of the college."

"Hoo hoo, Mr Baker! Mr Baker!"

"It begins with a toast round the sundial at two in the morning. The old fellas make a toast to time itself, which is followed by students walking backwards for an hour — time going backwards, you see? — balancing out time — which is basically an excuse for a piss up. Now I've got my own theory — "

"Hoo hoo, Mr Baker! Mr Baker!"

Mr Baker stopped talking at this point and turned gruffly to face the archway where the vicar stood, as if only now had the matter come to his attention.

"About this carol service, Mr Baker," said the vicar. *"The carol*

service? The organ? We are all waiting, you know."

Mr Baker straightened up to deliver his reply.

"Shut your mouth you bald headed goat," he shouted at the vicar, poking his walking stick in the night air. "You sir are a rude man."

The vicar sputtered and wavered, but nothing coherent came out of his mouth. It simply opened and closed by way of protest. By which point Mr Baker had his back to him anyway, explaining to Sandra more about the regular passage of time and space.

Then he asked her what it was she was studying. He rolled his eyes at the reply, at the prospect of book keeping. But he liked Sandra's accent, and considered it refreshing. When she told him about the metaphysical poets, far preferable to a course in book keeping, Mr Baker stopped her short and re-cited something.

The Sun-beames in the East are sped,
Leave, leave faire Bride, your solitary bed

Fresh flecks of snow were on his nose.
"John Donne," said Sandra.
"John Donne," said Mr Baker.

"I think I may have blown my tipple this year." Mr Baker was referring to the bottle of port from the college cellar, usually given to him as payment for his services. He slumped at the realisation, watching the vicar flee the scene like a character from a strip in the *Beano*, his face big and angry. The two students also made good their escape, leaving only Mr Baker and Sandra Setters standing by the Christmas tree. For a moment nothing was said between them. Looking up at the sky, Sandra watched the snow fall and then Mr Baker asked whether she had ever seen the Uffington White Horse.

The question was a surprise. The Uffington White Horse?

Sandra was in for a treat. Off they went to Uffington in Faringdon, Mr Baker driving an old motor car, three times over the legal limit. It took a good hour to get to there. But it was too dark to see anything on White Horse Hill when they arrived, no sign of the equestrian Bronze Age figure carved into the hillside. The horse looked to have bolted, so Mr Baker filled in the details.

"In good light," he said, "it is possible to stand here and see ancient history. Ancient history in the here and now, so to speak. Here we have the White Horse, which can be seen for miles, except now we can't see it, of course."

Mr Baker had a torch. He shone it at his head as he tapped his temple.

"Quite something," he said.

Then he directed the weak beam of light further up the hill, illuminating a few more feet of snow.

"The Giant's Steps are up there. Rivulets in the ground created by the retreating Ice Age. A castle too. It's the highest point in Oxfordshire up there. And we are surrounded by burial sites. From Neolithic times. From Saxon times."

Mr Baker considered the world surrounding them. It was black because it was night, but it was also white because it was covered in snow. And this is what history is like, said Mr Baker.

Sandra smiled. He talked like no one else she knew.

"Legends of St George slaying the dragon," he then said, shining the torch in a different direction, as if knowing of the precise spot. "Nothing remains of either of them — St George, the dragon — and nothing more of the castle. But there they are. Listen."

Sandra strained her eyes and ears. There was nothing out of the ordinary but the moment was magical.

Cast your mind back to that ridiculous skirt.

She walked to the end of the street to the front door that was his door — number 36 — and knocked on it. It was cold and the wind was blowing.

On the high street in the distance she could see tourists posing for photographs in front of something old and suitably British. They wore cravats and coats with high collars, and arranged themselves for their instamatic cameras. She watched them until the door rattled open and Mr Baker was there as if he had been waiting behind it the whole time.

He was very happy to see her again, and waved her in.

In the hallway was a collection of crystal glass with commemorative names on them. He took her coat and hung it up, then pulled the curtain closed behind the door to keep the draft out and led the way down the hallway to the living room at the back of the house.

He made small talk, asking her about her pending exams. She made a dismissive remark.

She enjoyed the company of Mr Baker. Mr Baker, she called him, although he had insisted on that first meeting it would have to be Rhodri, plain and simple, because there was no standing on formalities here, he said.

Nice Mr Baker. He had thin grey hair and the house the fuzz of men who do not leave it often. He made his way round with the aid of a walking stick, padding the carpet with a *tup tup* sound. In the living room with its brown furniture and gas fire the smell of nicotine was strong and the music he liked was playing. Mr Baker stood for a moment holding onto the mantle-shelf as if it was high time to make a decision. With a start he hobbled over to the record deck to turn the music off.

"Please, no. I like it," said Sandra. "What is it?"

"You do? Cavalli. The opera *La Rosinda*." He affected an Italian accent.

Mr Baker let the record play, but turned down the volume a notch. "Hear ourselves think," he said. He put the empty record sleeve back on the shelf, in its place. Nice Mr Baker. Meticulous Mr Baker.

Cast your mind back to that ridiculous skirt.

Mr Baker had this habit of fidgeting with his thumbs, as happened when he spoke about gypsy fortune tellers on the promenade in Blackpool, or the Black and White Minstrels on the television, or when there was something disagreeable on his mind.

Divination by the tarot was a serious business, he said. No time for hokum. He invited Sandra over because he could show her a few things. He was anxious to get his point across and he rolled his thumbs. The table in the middle of the room was already laid out with its deck of cards placed in the middle, wrapped in a red scarf as it had been the week before.

From the top of the deck Mr Baker took a card and placed it with care face-up on the table. It happened to be The Fool. He looked at the card a moment before repeating the pattern until on the table he had placed ten cards.

"We read these cards much the same way we do the Celtic Cross," he said. His finger traced the pattern of the cards. On the final sweep his finger caught the tablecloth and disgorged the triangles from the tree of the Qabala. Some of the cards fell to the floor.

"Oh, my dear," said Mr Baker.

Sandra jumped from her chair to pick the cards up, thus saving Mr Baker the trouble. He might do himself an injury bending over at his age. She was on her knees returning the cards to their place on the table, saying how it wasn't a problem.

Mr Baker said something altogether different in return. She didn't quite catch it. But otherwise there was no indication of the neuroses, the anxieties, the ribald pleasure that bubbled beneath the surface that afternoon; no indication of the transformation taking place.

When Sandra finished collecting the cards — it didn't take long — Mr Baker was nowhere to be seen. She was alone in the living room. She was alone for what may have been ten minutes. The record had reached the end and was locked in the run-out groove, clicking. Eventually Sandra poked her head into the hallway, ready to call upstairs to see if everything was alright. But then footsteps sounded on the landing and she dashed back to the chair at the table and sat down in a manner that made her feel it had been wrong to leave the room in the first place.

He had been Mr Baker — nice Mr Baker — and now he was coming down the stairs.

"I have been somewhat naughty," came the voice that sounded like his. It was much more firm than it was before, and she noticed it was without the accompaniment of the *tup tup* sound of the walking stick, the sound that accompanied Mr Baker everywhere. Indeed it wasn't Mr Baker who was approaching at all. The light on the landing cast a shadow on the wall that was on all fours.

"Did you see what I was doing?" said the voice that wasn't Mr Baker. It was a singsong kind of a voice. "See the man who is looking? See the man who is looking?"

Sandra Setters was not able to speak. The shadow that anticipated the thing that was coming had paused to shake the tip its head as if it might howl. It didn't howl. It said: "He had a roll-up and while it didn't look like he was up to much he said he was."

It continued ambling down the stairs and Sandra, who didn't know what else to do, placed her hands flat on the table and waited.

The thing that arrived in the doorway was a horse. Rather it was Mr Baker on his hands and knees behaving like a horse. He was wearing a joke shop horse's head that had big immobile eyes and a mane of ginger hair running down its neck. The neck was tucked into the colourful prayer towel from India, wrapped round like a jaunty cravat. His shirt and jacket were gone, as was his trousers. In their place a long brown skirt with a bold paisley pattern on it.

Mr Baker rose slowly to his feet as if only then had he discovered the ability to do so. Tall and erect he applied movement to his new upstanding status and walked clumsily into the room.

"I must apologise, Ms Setters," said Mr Baker. "I should have warned you."

The words were muffled behind the mask. But they were singsong words. Suddenly Sandra was most amused. She snorted a laugh and clutched a hand to her mouth to stifle it, thinking it rude to laugh at Mr Baker. She considered his words and said at last something quite ineffectual, "I don't think it matters. I knew it was you."

The horse with its fixed expression requested a story. It wanted Sandra to read to it a story from the notebook on the shelf next to the record albums. Sandra took the notebook from the shelf and turned it over in her hands. The notebook was a few years old. It was scuffed and the edges worn, and it more resembled a ledger of accounts, but inside on every page was a story, each exquisitely written in blue ink with a fountain pen. She had no doubt the author was Mr Baker.

The horse pointed out the story it wanted to hear. It was on a page marked by a ribbon. Then it snuggled beneath the living room table, making itself comfortable as if it was in was a stable. Sandra began to read, tentatively at first. When the horse whinnied approval on hearing Sandra's northern brogue she was a lot more confident and read without further pause.

The story — its title in block capitals — *The Ormskirk Writing Circle* — was a story about a horse. All the stories in the notebook were stories about a horse in some capacity, as Sandra was to discover in the coming weeks.

When the story was finished Mr Baker returned, in as much as he took off the horse's head and said he was hungry. He wasn't able to get out much. Moreover he wanted Sandra to escort him into town where he would pay for a slap-up meal. The least he could do. He was very specific; he wanted to go to the Golden Cross Restaurant on Cornmarket Street. Apparently he had some history there. He whinnied when Ms Setters agreed.

They got ready. Upstairs in his bedroom she found clothes to replace that ridiculous skirt, but he wanted the horse's head back on, so off they went together holding hands like barnyard friends, the student Sandra Setters and Mr Baker the horse. It was raining but they had an umbrella and were classy. It was dark but they were classy. After the restaurant they sat on a bench outside Freeman, Hardy & Willis where they talked about the stars.

THE ORMSKIRK WRITING CIRCLE

The prompts arrived in the mail, nine manila envelopes, each addressed to a member of the group. I found the local post office on the first morning following our arrival at the cottage in Cornwall. Arthur had mailed the prompts earlier in the week, as he did whenever members of the Ormskirk Writing Circle went off on one of its literary soirees.

I grabbed all but the new girl's envelopes. She wore a Qajar dress from Iran, although she was from Ormskirk. She insisted that she take her envelope right away and tore it open there and then, in the street. Each member of the group had a differ-

ent prompt for a story, which, when finished, would be read out and feedback given. The new girl laughed when she read her prompt. But she would not let anyone see it.

I did not open my envelope. My prompt could wait.

As happened each year, members of the group booked a house for a weekend retreat. The house was always someplace different, albeit a remote location that was connected in some shape or form to a famous author or a literary scene. One year it was Robin Hood's Bay, near to Whitby, the inspirational home for Bram Stoker's Dracula. *Another year it was Haworth, West Yorkshire, the birthplace of the Brontë sisters.*

The retreats were always exciting and fun. We did decadent things and conducted literary experiments in the hills. We even invented a motto in Latin, which looked fancy but translated to "We urinate on your gowns." This because Ormskirk was not Cambridge or Oxford. It was all done in good humour.

The cottage in Cornwall was associated with the novelist Daphne Du Maurier, who had lived most of her life in the nearby village of Fowey.

I was at a window that overlooked the courtyard, where a horse was tethered. The horse wore a saddle on its back. At first I thought the saddle was moss, like a wooden handrail left open to the elements. But no, it was a saddle...

Sandra Setters did not stop reading the story, but, lifting her eyes, she saw the agitation it was causing in the listener. Something had spooked the horse in the tale and Mr Baker beneath the table reacted in kind. She continued reading.

It was the neighbour's silly dog. It had escaped and was running through the courtyard. Panicked the magnificent horse reared up and broke its tether. It kicked out wildly, striking the farmer's vintage motor car, which was on blocks in need of repair.

Consequently the vintage motorcar rolled away, following the incline of the courtyard to the farmhouse — towards the window through which I observed everything — and crashed into a wall that had been rendered only a week ago.

At this point in the story, Mr Baker started to laugh. He was still on the floor, his arms folded on his raised knees. He rocked on his backside as he laughed. When it seemed he had finished laughing, Sandra returned to the story. But Mr Baker was not finished laughing, he started over again, so while she made an attempt to pick up the story again, she felt it improper to speak over Mr Baker, being old like he is and under the living room table.

"Motor car," Mr Baker tittered, shaking his large horse's head.

Sandra avoided Mr Baker. She couldn't put it into words, but something was broken between them, and the visits thereafter got less and less, until one day she failed to show up at his door altogether. It was getting to be quite the same anyway: ten minutes after her arrival, Mr Baker would become a horse and she would read to it another one of his stories — none made sense, nor were they particularly well written.

She surprised even herself when she plunged into the study of sums, becoming the poster girl for the department. She found it easy to avoid Mr Baker. After all, he was retired and almost never came to visit the college. He was disgraced as an organist, so he never came to the chapel either. Shouting at the vicar was the stuff of legend.

The last time that she bumped into him was in Blackwell's. It was hardly bumping into him, more like seeing him and running away. It was some months after her last visit to his house. She found herself wandering through the bookshop from the top floor down, as sometimes she did on an afternoon. On the lower ground floor was Mr Baker, beneath a wool hat, crooked over his walking stick. He was at the far end of the room, in the theology section. Sandra was headed that way, but stopped short when she saw him. From behind a bookcase she peered at him, unsure whether he had yet seen her. Then she turned on her heels and left without as much as a goodbye.

That was long ago.

Now Sandra Setters is celebrating her pending marriage to a man called Timothy Lomax with a weekend hen party in London. The memory of Mr Baker that was faded like old jeans had never left her completely and sometimes she thought of those strange afternoons, in the brown living room that smelled of nicotine, when Mr Baker excused himself and then returned. Odd Mr Baker. In a pub on the Old Kent Road the memory came back in a way that made her dizzy.

Sandra was slumped over a line of cocktail glasses, some empty. It was mid-evening in pub #3 and the Mint Julip showed no sign of running dry any time soon, her girls were making sure of it.

"This is terrible," said Sandra. "I'm having a terrible time."

But no one could hear her over the cacophony of the party, which was tightly grouped in an annex of the pub. A sign on the door of the annex euphemistically referred to it as The Library. The girls didn't look much like they were in a library. They wanted to dance, shrieking with delight at everything that was spoken between them.

Why did they have to be so loud? Sandra thought. It reminded her why she rarely hung out with her friends any more. This wasn't her idea of a good time, and she sat away from them, at a table by herself.

Sandra turned her woozy attention elsewhere, to the brass plaques hanging on the wall, which looked like the things a show horse might wear. Then she cast her eyes over the tatty books that lined the shelves, a totally random collection that looked to have been acquired from Oxfam as a job lot.

Then the neon drinks sign above her started to flicker, its light casting a whole new design of solitude. "The library," she snorted and grabbed a book at random from the shelves. It had no spine. It was *The Oxford Dictionary of Allusions*. She turned to a section in the book on solitude. It gave examples of solitary individuals, among them Robin Crusoe, Greta Garbo, Howard Hughes, Ishmael and Jesus. Then to a section on horses. Black Beauty, Pegasus, Rosinante, and Sleipnir. Then a section on sound.

She stopped reading and looked at her friends. They were tired leper women swaying to their own cacophonous laughter. Fancy handbags at their feet resembled fluffy old dogs.

Sandra rose unsteadily to her feet, but loud enough to be heard this time.

Her friends made fantastic noises as they came to her with hugs and explained how it was perfectly normal to feel anxious because it was such an important day marrying Timothy, who was nice. (They couldn't stretch to calling him "hot" or even much of a catch.) They reminded her she was having fun.

Sandra was not having fun, far from it. In that moment she wanted to shape-shift. She wanted the bones of her back to arch and crack and form anew as a dog or cat or something from the Bronze Age, and she wanted her sinews to become beautiful creatures, like leaping lizards. She did not want to be on the Old Kent Road ensconced in sequins in the company of others whose bright pink sashes carried slogans that rhymed old china with vagina. She was at the precipice of years and years of normal service and she did not like it.

"Balls to this," she said, and took a swipe at the Mint Julip that sent it flying from the table in a most satisfying way.

Sandra excused herself from the room. Her manner made it clear that she was not likely to return any time soon. Despite some of the girls attempting to corral her back to the pub, she was having none of it. Goodnight, she said. She was returning to her hotel on the Euston Road.

Sandra thought about this marriage. She thought that perhaps it would best to call Timothy Lomax and tell him she couldn't go through with it. She considered doing this, and a lot of other things that evening. She wanted to raid the minibar. But she did not. At some point she turned out the light and slept.

In the morning, with dawn peeking through the blinds, Sandra sat up on the top of the bed to see the party girl back in the mirror. The pathetic specimen of only a few hours ago seemed not so pathetic anymore. Life, the woman before her seemed to say, is not linear but dances like oil on water, coalescing one minute before slowly wending new paths in the next.

So Sandra sees in the mirror one path of her future in which she marries Timothy Lomax and they have a life together, and children — two girls — who she adores. But never does she write any poetry. Those metaphysical poets she once admired seem silly now. Donne had been her favourite.

The paths continue to diverge. When Sandra grows old and dies only the tears fall. There is not a public holiday to mark her passing. Nobody outside her immediate neighbours on Queens Hill Crescent, Chippenham, even know she is gone, and fewer still remember much about her at all. Her friends remember only the hint of indiscretion, the hen party that ended so badly and that rumour about her college days. There was an odd fellow she had known at Merton. Old, he was old. That was the trouble with Sandra Setters, they will say, needing no further elaboration.

Sandra Setters does marry Timothy Lomax, but she also

writes poetry. And one day she travels back to Oxford, to the house that was Mr Baker's house, number 36. She knocks on the door, half expecting in the swirl of past and present that an old man with a walking stick will answer and he will say "My dear girl," before kissing her lightly on the cheek.

MY LOVE, MY LIFE

Megan Davis

I first notice my love on the bus to work. A beautiful man, gorgeous enough to rival even me. He sits across the aisle, staring into space. Occasionally his gaze flicks over to me and then quickly away. He is dressed for work in a business suit, tidy and stiff. He gets off at my stop and I do not see him again until much later.

Whilst I am performing my nightly pampering routine, playing idly on my phone, my love comes up on a dating app. His face displays a crooked half-smile. His favourite activities are sex and watching TV. It transpires we share a name. How I laugh at this revelation. My love is so compatible with me that I ache for him.

No one could ever tempt me like my love. I am stunning, heavenly, iridescent. Once, a woman tried to seduce me. I laughed in her face whilst she cried. She did not deserve me.

My love reappears when I am wearing my dark blue duffle coat, the one that broadens my shoulders. I glimpse him from across the shopping mall, before we are both swept aside by strangers. I catch his slight smile; my love recognises me too. In that brief moment, his beauty swells tenfold. I am amazed, and aroused. I thought I was perfect, but perhaps — perhaps this man might be also.

At a club, at a friend of a friend of a friend's birthday party, there my love is again. I instruct the host but when she tries to find him, he has vanished. Later, on the dancefloor, my love joins me. I ask where he went, but he smiles and laughs, and I laugh and smile, and we dance. His skin is soft and cold.

We have dinner in a fancy restaurant. I carry a daffodil in my lapel. The food is delicious and my love and I delight in each other's company. The other patrons stare at us as we eat, and we relish the attention, their clear envy. I am in love with this man, for he is glorious. We are unparalleled.

Later I spy another man checking him out as we walk through the town together. I am bitterly jealous. My love is mine, mine, mine. I want us to run home immediately, and so we do, and we arrive breathless and exhilarated.

One evening I whisper to my love that we might stay at home forever so that no one can steal him away. I implore, I beg, I plead. We make a blanket fort and huddle in the cosy warmth.

I long to spend all my time with him; my love, my light, my life. I want to look at his face forever, to feel the cold touch of his skin beneath my fingers, to press my cheek against his cheek and catch the laugh in his smile. I want to be with him and him alone and forget the world. I know he feels the same.

I lock the doors and shut the curtains and guard against those who would seek to take my love from me. We cling together, my love and me. We are all we need.

We spend a month like this, isolated from society. The cupboards are in need of replenishment and we have not seen daylight in almost a fortnight, but I cannot bear to part from my love, pressed close as we are to one another. I cannot risk another stealing him away from me, so we hide in the dark, apart from everyone else.

My grip is weak and I can barely stand, but my love does

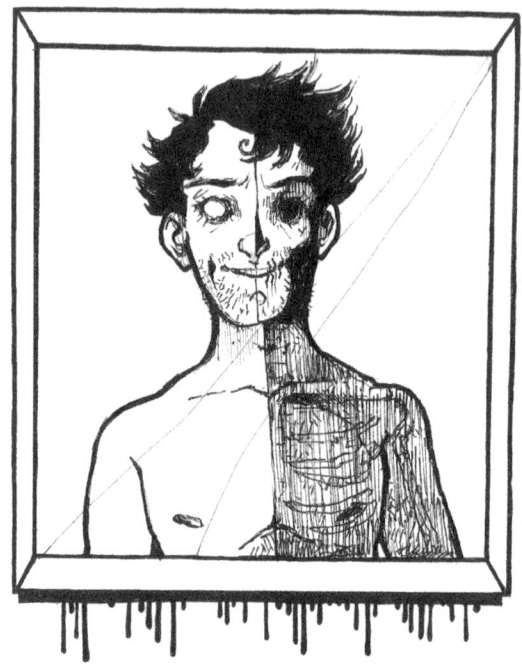

not leave me. We lean upon each other for support. He is still perfect.

They find my body a week later. It has wasted away; filthy, decomposing and ugly. The mirror I am propped against is smeared from the pressing of my skin on glass. My eyes are still open, hollow and dark, holding the gaze of my love forevermore.

LOVE IN THE LEAVES

Hannah Dade

"What kind of idiot goes for a picnic in winter?" He removes each of the plastic containers from his bag and places them beside him, in height order. There are lines of frost where the sun doesn't touch the slats of the bench.

She pours tea from a flask. "You've only got yourself to blame. Twenty-two-year-old you, but you nonetheless."

"It was cheap. I suppose I thought it'd be romantic." He grips the tupperware clips but can't pry them open. His hands aren't what they were, blasted things, and the cold doesn't help. Inside are four reduced-fat, off-brand cheese spread sandwiches, cut into triangles for a special occasion. They jostle a bit as he uses the bench arm for leverage, the box popping open with a creak. And there it is, the scent of that first date together. "There was that thing you wanted to look at too, some rocks or something."

"Wharram Brock." She corrects him. "It's not rocks, it's an abandoned village."

"Well, we never found it."

"I'm not convinced it actually exists." She opens her sandwich and adds a layer of salt and vinegar crisps. It's best to add them just before eating, otherwise the texture is all wrong.

Geese, ducks, and coots waddle over to investigate their

food, chuffing and wagging their tails. The forest houses both native species and some prettier ones escaped from ornamental duck ponds, all of them unafraid of people. Years ago, when Oliver was knee-height, they'd brought him here to fill those endless summer days, with bread to feed them. That was before they knew bread was harmful to ducks, and before the visitor centre was built. There was a carpark now, too. They could both remember when this was just fields. At least it's easier to drive.

Trees had deferred for woodchip paths and a children's play area. Oaks still stood sentinel over the play apparatus, willow branches had been bent and manipulated to make an archway which burst into greens during the warm months. The forest adjusted around the life inside it.

They both pat the back of the bench before leaving and thank George, to whom it's dedicated. The frost obscures the inscription but they know it so well. A pale brindled moth resting here bats its wings and flies away. The cold doesn't affect it as it does the other animals, it doesn't freeze and so these months are its domain. It seeks out a female, she will be wingless and somewhere among the treetops.

"Do you remember that time with Oliver and the stag beetle?" The man laughs.

How could she forget? Oliver, now a sensible person with starched-collars who took business lunches in the city, had found a particularly large stag beetle. He'd been so proud of his find that he'd eaten it. They'd driven him to A&E and waited four hours to be told he'd be fine. "Can you even imagine him *touching* a beetle now?"

They come to the bridge. It's older now, in need of repair. Sunlight glimmers in tiny pinpricks, a whisper of frost. Fungi prickle out the darkest corners, with speckles of moss and lichen, light lines work across the wood in echoes of plant roots once attached here. A squirrel bounds onto the railing and up a nearby birch.

A man dressed in a polo shirt and bare arms is cutting back the bracken. "Alright?" He calls to them. He is known in the area, practically absorbed into the landscape itself, ubiquitous with the forest. He worked here as a lad, and they couldn't be rid of him even in retirement. "Careful on that bridge, someone made a complaint the other week. They tripped on the wonky step, said it should be sign-posted." Everyone agrees that people aren't as sensible as they used to be, health and safety gone mad.

As the couple continue their walk, the warden is packing away his things. He has a habit of singing to himself, nonsense songs mostly. They bounce off the trees and the grass and the leaves. There are shears attached to his belt, a ring of keys for the visitor centre, the toilets, and the sheds.

He was here when the family sold the land and left it to the wilds. They'd thought that would be the best. Then they realised that they had a patch of nettles with an occasional oak tree, that it wasn't just a case of leaving things to grow, and they gifted it to a Trust to manage. Back then there were fewer red kites. He loves kites, loves watching them hover in the sky before sweeping down. There are less of most things now, but the kites were thriving. Their cries are a beautiful sound.

A river gurgles under that wonky bridge. River is a generous word for what this is, more a brook, but it was once a river and so a river it remains to the land, even if it has trickled to such a small size that the little surface that remains freezes in the winter. Some years it can disappear entirely, retreat into the riverbanks fat with larvae, ready to burst into a mist of insects. Other times it seems to have boundless energy, the sun dancing on pebbles in a cascade of colours, dancing off the surface which might be disturbed by pond skaters or the occasional vole. Now it slept. It was a murk of darkness and slowness, its inhabitants slow while they awaited the glut to come.

It had been a grand thing, back when the forest was still, and no humans disturbed the undergrowth. Not that there was peace; the soundscape of this land had always been one of vehemence and energy, the screeching threats of birds, the cacophony of mating calls and declarations of territory, the sudden thrash of predator against prey, squeals of indignation and terror.

The land remembers. It remembers beyond that, too. It remembers a time before humans and a time after humans, when the undergrowth claws back its domain, when the only sound that punctuates the quiet are the guttural calls of deer. It remembers everything at once, things that have happened, things that might, things that probably never would. A time when the visitor centre will be dismantled and crumble, when the river will fade entirely, when the skies turn to longer winters, or else no winters at all.

A greyhound presses its nose to the river and gulps mouthfuls of muddy water. Its human calls "no, not the- oh Christ on a bike," she has a bottle in her hands, one that folds out to become a bowl. She pats the dog on its neck.

"Afternoon," the warden says. "Remember to keep dogs on a lead."

"Right. Sorry." The woman bows her head a little as she apologises. She moved to the area eight months ago and has only recently started coming here. She clips her greyhound to its lead, but she disagrees with the concept and will release it as soon as the warden turns his back.

The dog's ears prick. It lifts its neck and stares. Then bolts. It has seen a squirrel. The lead pulls taut and yanks the woman after her dog.

"No, Garnet, no!" She cries as she drops the lead. "Come back!"

The squirrel climbs to safety. It has a peanut in its paws, pilfered from the bird feeders. It's grey and fat, despite the season. It eats the nut within view of the greyhound, an ineffectual predator.

There is a cluster of bird feeders near the visitor centre, above a manmade pond. There is a window next to it, the glass marked where children have placed their faces against it. Posters line the walls with images of creatures and plants that inhabit the forest, their frenetic energy somehow caught in watercolour illustrations. There is no one inside today, except the mice and bats that have made their homes in the bricks and the roof.

A great tit clings to a wire frame. It has lived its whole life in this patch of woods, all of two years. For two years it has watched squirrels paw through the seeds and the fat balls. For two years it has learnt the footsteps of those that replenish the feeders, learnt the rattle of the seed bucket, its entire existence has been in tandem with this small garden within the forest. It bathes in the manmade pond and when it was a hatchling it rested in a nest made of moss and feathers and discarded plastic. Its ancestors nested here and its descendants will nest here, in boxes constructed for them, in cups they constructed, in what will remain of the shed, within that building once all the posters are removed.

The forest covers all with its branches, in its memories of things that have been and those that have not yet. It has had its moments, had its nights of weakness. There were the fires. It remembers the groups of riders that used to run through here, hunting boar; it remembers the primal fear in that boar's eye and it had tried to protect it. It remembers their shouts. And further back, to a time of wolves. It feels their pulsing fear, their constant anxiety, the constant balance of peril and delight.

In a world claimed by the fungus and the spores and all other beneficiaries of rot and decay. The worms will eat what remains, life growing from life, the waters will wash away the silt as the sea is reunited with the earth. Simultaneously it claims it, it freezes, it retreats, and there is just the trees and a couple celebrating the passage of time.

The songbirds will nest in what remains of the trees, if the land remembers correctly. They will eat further generations of moths, grown black from the environment.

A time will come when the visitor centre will close, a time when it has been closed for countless years. Plants will push through the road leading here, first through the stone path and then through the concrete.

Still then the land will nurture them, it will nurture everything within it. It is the heartbeat of the mayflies, the spiders, the worms, the butterflies. It is the nervous system of the trees and the plants, beating life to everything within its soils. It nurtures the mammals, the rodents, the badgers, the deer, even the humans. And when everything is turned to naught but spores of a fungus, it will live on even then.

It loves the creatures in it, and always has.

MUTE

Jess Hyslop

I still can't make head nor tail of it. Is that surprising? I don't think that's surprising. I mean, is there honestly another guy out there — I mean a normal guy, a guy like me, a guy with an it-kinda-sucks-but-it'll-do job and a beat-up car and, OK, a little bit of a beer gut coming on — is there a guy like that who can honestly say that he'd come home to his dead wife watching TV on the couch and *not* be kinda messed up by it?

So when I say dead, I don't mean that she looks dead, not like she's a rotting corpse or anything zombie-movie-style like that. Because that's just the thing: I come in on a Tuesday night, a little late on account of stopping by the store on the way home, and she's just sitting there, watching that crappy show — you know, the one with that presenter with plastic-looking hair and scarily white teeth — with her legs tucked up under her like she always used to do. And I just stand there like an idiot with the grocery bag in my hand, and then I just kinda go "Lucy?" Just like that. "Lucy?"

I don't know what I'm expecting, because jeez, but she just turns her head and looks at me, and she looks just the same, you know? Just the same as before, as, you know, before she died. And then she just goes, "Hey", and turns back to the TV. I mean, I'm still standing there like oh-my-holy-crap-you're-dead-though and she just goes back to watching that stupid plastic-hair guy. So now I'm trying to think of what to say, and then it occurs to me that maybe she doesn't know she's dead? Like maybe for her this is just like any other Tuesday night? And so I reckon, OK, I've gotta say something.

So I say, "But you're dead." Which, OK, looking back on it now it sounds kinda stupid, especially if she didn't know she was dead, because can you imagine if you were just sitting there watching TV, thinking everything was normal, and then your husband comes home and goes "Hey, but you're dead." I mean, that would freak me the fuck out, if it were the other way round.

Luckily, though, it seems like she must have known, because she just kinda looks at me and shrugs like a little *what can you do?* shrug and just goes straight back on watching her show.

And, I don't know, it seems weird, but her reacting like that, like it was no big deal her coming back from the dead, that kinda made me react like it was no big deal either. So even though in my head I'm still all like what-the-fuck, outside I find I'm doing an *OK, no biggie* shrug right back at her. And then, get this, I'm stepping right past her, doing a mumbled "Sorry" as I get in front of the TV, and I'm going into the kitchen and putting away the groceries like nothing has happened.

I'm there for maybe a minute or so, and then this chirpy little tune sounds from the lounge, which tells me her show is finished, and when I turn around, there she is. Just standing in the doorway, leaning on it with her head on one side, watching me.

"Hey," she says. "Good day?"

"S'all right," I say. And in my head I'm asking her all these questions like: What the actual fuck? But you were dead! We had a funeral at St. Mary's and the Browns' youngest kid puked on his shoes just when the priest was doing his sermon bit, so everyone had to fish around for tissues to wipe the puke off, and I was so pissed that he'd puked at your funeral — like couldn't he have picked another time, like any other time, to puke? And how the heck did you even get back here looking like that, like everything is OK, like normal? Is there an empty grave in that churchyard now that you clawed your way out of? And does your mom know, because your mom's going to blow a gasket when she finds out, might even be the end of her and wouldn't that be ironic? And anyway, are you staying? Are you back for good now?

But while I'm thinking all this, there she is, just padding round the kitchen in her pyjamas and bare feet, wrinkling her nose at the beer cans in the sink, which I meant to throw out but, OK, hadn't got around to yet. She goes up on tiptoe to look in the cupboard, and rummages a bit, and then looks at me with this disappointed pouty face she does. Did. Whatever.

"We're out of cocoa."

"Shoot," I say. "I musta forgot about cocoa." And why do I even say that, when I know the whole time I never buy cocoa now because I don't drink it, only she drank cocoa. But still I do this kinda *oops, I screwed up* face and go, "You want cocoa? I can go back now and get some."

"No, don't worry, babe. It's OK."

But she says it in that tone of voice that says it's not really OK, so I say, "No, sure, it's fine, I'll get it, won't take five minutes."

And then I'm shoving my wallet back in my pocket and heading back through the lounge to the front door. She's left the TV on again like she always does, did, and I'm fed up of telling her not to because of how it runs up the bills, and still I find myself saying, "Hey, turn that off, will ya?" like I always do, did, ugh.

She sighs and grabs the remote and switches it on mute, and looks at me like *OK, that good enough?* And, well, you know, the sound wasn't really the point, but I don't want to have a fight about the stupid TV, especially not tonight, what with her having just risen from the grave and all. So I just say, "OK, won't be long," and then I go out again and get in the car.

And you know the weirdest thing? The weirdest thing of all is: what do I do next? Do I go tell someone or go to the police or to my best mate Mike or to my neighbour or anyone and go, hey, help me, Lucy's back and she's watching TV in our lounge like nothing is wrong and I am freaking right out here? The fuck I do. I just drive straight down to the store again and pick out some cocoa, and when I go to pay the cashier says, "Forgot something, ha ha?" and I just go, "Yeah, what a dope, right? Ha ha." And if she recognises it's the brand that Lucy always liked, that I haven't bought for six months because why would I, she doesn't say nothing about it.

So here I am, sat in my car, back outside my house — *our house* — and I'm kinda wondering is this real? Only the thing is, I can hear the TV again even from here, so someone must have turned the sound back on, and where that blue-white TV light is pulsing through the curtains, I can see a silhouette where someone's standing there and flicking through the channels.

And I gotta say, I'm sitting here staring at my hands on the steering wheel, trying to think through this whole mess, and I still can't make head nor tail of it. But the thing is, my wife's in there and she wants this cocoa, which right now is just lying here on the passenger seat, so I ask you, I mean, what else can a guy like me do?

THE MEMORALABE

Alexander Walker

If you're reading this, then I have given it away. Perhaps for the best, but we won't get into that now. If you have it, take caution and, when you get there, follow my grandfather's advice. You'll have questions, lord knows I did, but I asked them too late.

It had been in the loft all along, once tucked behind a stack of old newspapers, now fallen and wedged between the eaves. My grandfather was a hoarder and the columns of junk, or rather, of memories given form, stretched taller than I. The years had not been kind, columns lay bent or toppled, and spilled their nostalgic guts to the wooden floor. Dust and cobwebs covered everything like snow. Except this snow was more apt to make you sneeze.

I remember I'd wriggled far enough to consider turning back, clothes already dusted and creased from debris. When I was a child it had been a veritable playground of tunnels and caves, walls painted with imagination as we rifled through lost treasures and trinkets. Now a grown man it was considerably more difficult to navigate a space now known only as a crypt for the junk of a dead old man.

This time, however, I was after something specific.

Grandfather's hidden treasure had been often whispered as a family rumour but when he'd throw a fit, which was often in his waning years, it was all he'd ever shout about.

Now though, I was convinced I would find it. After all, the letter said it would be here. The chest lay wedged under a scattering of newspapers that had most articles removed. It was small but incredibly heavy. The ornate keyhole on the front marked the lid as locked. I had the key, it had been enclosed in the letter addressed to me following my grandfather's wishes. Outside of confirmation of its existence and its exact location all the letter said was, '*Use it sparingly and don't end up like me*'.

As I lay horizontal I wrestled free the key from my pocket, rolled in dust and squeezed my arm through a gap of fallen stacks. It clicked with satisfaction.

It was gold, I knew it would be, still shiny and well polished. A thick golden disc wrapped in a velvet sash. I took the treasure from its hiding place, leaving the key in the open chest like a burst oyster robbed of its pearl. I clutched it to myself as I wriggled back, now uncaring for the mounds of dust that spilled and soiled my clothes. I couldn't wait to see it.

After gathering a few things; a glass of water, a notebook, a pen, I unwrapped it on the dining room table. The house lay empty, grandmother now occupying my own childhood room after grandfather passed. And my house where the footfalls of my own children spelled almost immediate danger just would not do. This place, however, was on pause. Suitably furnished but unlived and unloved. No food in a fridge, nor flowers in a vase.

I unwrapped it diligently. From its velvet bed it looked up at me.

The *memoralabe*.

I sat before my knees gave out and set the chunky disc on

its edge like an undecided coin. Delicately using both hands I clicked away the two faces from a central piece and laid them flat on each side like a butterfly resting in the sun. The insides of these faces were lidded but once removed revealed concave bowls burnt with soot. These were the braziers. The central piece was as intricate and ornate as any golden timepiece. Cogs of all sizes, both silver and gold, scattered its innards. There were no screws to speak of, no seams or panels and the engravings that littered any free space were in a language I did not recognise.

I set both lids to the side and blew scant ash from both braziers.

With one hand you give, with another you receive.

Excitedly, I tore a page from a notebook then tore that again in two.

Tokens could come in many forms: photographs, diary pages, newspaper clippings, even scribbles if the mind was clear.

I clicked the pen from my pocket and began to scribble animatedly.

The time Mel and I argued and she smashed a vase.

As I wrote it, I remembered it. The poky flat we shared, the leaky tap, that carpet turned up at the edges. A vase by a kitchen sink, her body leant against it, tense and angry.

"If you're not going to act like an adult then why don't you just — "

I shook myself loose of the spiral and dropped the paper into the left brazier before sliding the second scrap closer.

It doesn't matter which side you use but the order remains the same. First you give, then you receive.

I edged a box of matches from my pocket, the first one taking flame immediately. I held the match to the scrap and its edges took. Within thirty seconds it was ash.

I smiled, put the lid back with a magnetic pull and put the pen to paper again.

When I met Evie for the first time.

Again, it sparked some recollection.

The coffee shop. My work apron tassels. The chipped coffee mug, and the spill.

This scrap went in the brazier on the right. I filled it with water, the ink already starting to bleed and run. The lid sealed it inside.

I reset my rolled sleeves as the sweat broke. With both braziers fed I placed a hand under each face and began to close the memoralabe as I had always heard instructed. The cogs ratcheted and clicked. I felt each one through the golden faces. The innards spun at different speeds, louder clunks and clicks escaped. It closed with a firmer click and then began to whir. It seemed to draw power from something even without wires or batteries. Something else inside that turned on or unwound as it performed its archaic, arcane purpose.

Its thick rim bore small windows into the labe which soon began to glow, the gold becoming hot to the touch. Inside something was aflame. It trembled slightly. Clicking and whirring. Small pistons and pins seeming to peek out and recede back into the frame like an engine. For a moment I feared the thing might explode.

It began to whistle. An iris opened on its top. I was hesitant to peek over it but something called me all the same. It was the final stage.

I slid my chair back and stood, both hands on the table supporting me as I lowered my face over the iris. I held my face in a wince, ready to pull myself back at any moment. Steam poured forth as if from a kettle. I held firm.

I inhaled deeply. In through the nose, out through the mouth. Once, twice, a third time. By the end of the third breath the steam ended, the iris closed, the gold already beginning to cool. Silence. Nothing.

I sat and stared at the thing, now no instrument of arcane manipulation but a rather ornate paperweight.

I finished the glass of water and clicked the pen shut.

In the open notebook I had written, *Mel*.

I still knew what that meant. Not erased entirely, at least. I could see her face, except it felt further away. There was a significant moment but I couldn't recall. It hurt when I pushed for it, like a needle behind the eyes. No echo, no blur, only absence. I didn't need a scribble to remind me what to do next, I could still very much remember what I had written on the second note but minutes ago. *Evie*.

I didn't have to push, I barely had to think her name at all.

The table fell away, the walls blew out with white light and I jumped up out of the chair before I fell with it. When the light dimmed I was in the coffee shop. I stood behind the counter, apron tied tight, tassels swinging. A nozzle frothed milk. The room was full of indecipherable conversation. My hands worked a hot mug and towel before I noticed I could feel them. Every movement, every sight and every sound already predetermined. A carriage on the rails. Except this was a journey I had travelled before. My body jerked against my better judgement, these were judgments made by a much younger self, seeing through younger eyes. How they flickered hurriedly over details of each customer; eyes, mouth, scarf, shoes.

I was putting the mug down when I became aware of somebody on the other side of the counter. What hit me first was the smell of her perfume. My head jolted upward in a moment of instinct, or maybe reflex, my eyes dancing all the while. These moments were so short but on second viewing seemed to last twice as long. Eyes, mouth, scarf and shoes. She stood in many layers, windswept, steamed-over glasses obscuring her eyes. A huge scarf wrapped around her with one end trailing to a knee.

"Good afternoon. How can I help today?" I heard myself say. It was loud, like listening to music too high.

"Hiya, oh, excuse me, yes. Sorry..."

She removed her glasses and began clearing them on the scarf end.

I couldn't take my eyes off her. My hands, however, still on autopilot, misjudged the height of the counter and chipped the mug, spilling a shard to the floor.

I could feel my foot first quiet the shard and then slide it toward the bin. Slowly putting the mug down quietly and sliding it away. The whole moment was over in a second, maybe two, and what with the usual noise in the cafe I thought maybe I'd covered my error without her noticing as she fumbled with her things. The way she would later tell it I would know that I was wrong but in this moment, at least, I thought I'd got away with it.

"Just a coffee, thanks. Black," she said, readjusting her glasses.

I felt myself nod, nauseous in my own skull.

She handed me exact change and moved to a nearby table.

Unlike most memories, this one didn't speed up or skip the boring bits. I watched my younger hands as they prepped a new mug, turned on the machine, spilled the milk as I filled a small jug. It didn't skip the setting of the tray or the wiping down the surface, nor the cold clammy feeling of dishwater between fingers. I watched as I took the tray to the table. She sat, in what I remembered before as a beam of sunlight from a perfectly placed window. It was in fact just a spotlight, one of many on overhead runners, nothing unique or especially beautiful about it. No. She held all the beauty in the room already.

Her legs were crossed, the scarf trailed to the floor, her jacket hung from the chair. A leather bag lay agape, a notebook open and a pen scribbled avidly across its page.

"One black coffee," I felt myself say.

Again, distracted as my eyes lingered too long, the tray understepped its mark, setting down slightly short and in an over-correction moved too far and too swift causing the coffee to slosh and roll like the tides. Errant drops of it fled the mug with only one destination in mind. In my memory this happened in slow motion; trapped inside my skull it was over in a blink. A scatter of coffee drips peppered her page. Blue ink already starting to swirl in the golden smears as they faded into the paper. I felt a stone grow and then start to sink in my stomach.

"Oh my g— I am so sorry. Let me just..." I heard myself say, the limbs of my body moving with urgency as if on puppeteer's strings.

"It's fine...no, no...really..." she said behind me,

I grabbed paper towels from the front and returned, handing them to her apologetically.

"Really, it's no problem — thanks, really though, it's fine" she said,

"I am so sorry, miss, I hope that's not ruined anything important..."

"Just a shopping list," she said with a smile, taking a slow sip of the coffee as she patted the paper dry. Her eyes never left mine the whole time.

"Next coffee is on me, on the house, I mean, really, it's the least I can do."

"Thank you. That's very kind but really it's no trouble."

I felt my hands reach out and take the damp towels. I heard

customers waiting at the counter cough and clear throats trying to appear anything but impatient. I looked back at her and smiled and then I was right back in the living room. Still standing, hands on the table, breathing incredibly fast. It took a moment to remember where and even when I was. I looked at the memoralabe as I set my rolled sleeves to the elbow. *It really fucking works*, I thought.

After that I was hooked. Through trial and error I discovered a few stipulations; the time spans of both memories must be similar, an hour for an hour, a day for a day. Most recent memories were more readily available; older memories, though, needed something specific to hone in on. It would have been too easy to trade every grocery shop or toilet trip in my lifetime but while I knew I had done them, they were so inane I could no longer remember them specifically. At first, I was obsessed with saving the best bits, hours here and there from the very best days; the trips we took, holidays, special occasions, even those lazy weekends we never got out of bed. Back then I didn't worry about the cost, hours spent at work, fixing the car, a shit episode of a tv show. They all went down on paper, burnt in a brazier and merged with another in the memoralabe. Forgotten permanently, a hole punched out in my own mind.

Each memory that came back though, each one that I inhaled through the steam into my own skull, was a waking dream, only one that I would *never* forget. I could remember them as often as I liked, over and over again, picking up on every minute detail. And the best bit, they took no actual time to experience, hours on the sofa as we watched our favourite films came back to me in the blink of an eye. In the span of a single breath, an afternoon at a Christmas market, cream on our noses from the hot chocolates. In the time it took to button my shirt, the weekend we spent moving in together, debating where to put the mugs and where the tv should go.

It did wonders for my journal writing, I could relive memories over and over, in perfect clarity, never changing or fading, and never forgotten. It was with these journals I began to form a timeline. Starting with that first moment we met, when we never knew exactly how much we would fall in love. Each new memory led me to another, something said, something left on a table, or pinned to a wall. A photo of a holiday, printed out and soaked in the brazier. I could click my fingers and have spent a whole day on the coast, toes between sand and seas. An ice cream upturned in the dunes but we didn't care for all of the kisses we had instead.

I spent months doing this, one memory to another and so on. In the study journals filled up in secret. A near perfect timeline of our lives, yet, as the gaps began to close and fill there was only one direction to move, forward, and if I kept my course, it would not last long.

    I had forgotten which was the first bad day, I had an idea but really it had been sooner than I thought. A memory of a long drive I took the week before was written down and burnt, traded as if it was nothing. Two and a half hours, or thereabouts, I wish it had been less. That's when I realised this machine was just that — a machine. It traded like for like, time for time. Its purpose was not to recall only happiness, but truth. Two and a half hours, trapped in another hell. We were at her parents' place overlooking the sea. I was trying to scrape every last best minute I could for the journals, every side smile, every slow blink, every strand of hair tucked behind an ear. I remembered too late this was the first bad day. She sat on the sofa. She looked upset, her cup clinked in the saucer and she stood to move to the kitchen. Her leg gave out then, propped on one knee she coughed so hard she bled and —

Trapped in my own body, a rollercoaster ride of the worst kind. Feeling every panicked cry from my mouth, how cold my own blood ran, and the sweat. Awful cold clouds of it that weren't from exercise or exhaustion, no, they were from fear. Holding her hand in the back of an ambulance, in the sheer chaos of the moment, perhaps for the best, or maybe the worst, it ended.

There I was, sat in the study, Mel and the kids watching tv in the other room. That same cold cloud of sweat pouring out of me. Tears running tracks down my face and my lips shut tight for fear of spilling the lump in my throat. I looked at the memoralabe, now relocated to the study after I put the locks on. I started to think all at once this had been a terrible idea. I had never wanted to forget Evie, my first and only true love and the memoralabe had answered that call. After all, it was a gift. But now I would never forget. Those memories would not fade and change with time, those bad days would not get lost amongst the cracks. It was absolute, it was perfect, and it was love. All I had to do was blink my eyes, take a breath, button my fucking shirt, and I could be with her all over again.

And while that haunted me for a while, that wasn't the worst it would get. Remember those holes, punched out in my mind, well, there's an awful lot missing. *Use it sparingly* he'd said, but I didn't listen. You see, the longer I live, the more memories I make, the longer that internal film of memory runs, and the more those holes stretch and merge. I had to be rid of it. Eventually, if I ever lived to be as old as grandfather, I'd end up just like him, a lifetime of traded memories, another lifetime lost amongst the holes. A survivor wandering the wreckage of my own mind, no doubt throwing my own fit when I can't remember my own name, or where I am, or who I'm with.

To many that image is the last they have of him, however, I could do one better. The very last time I used the memoralabe I remembered him at his best. That spritely old man who still had life in his eyes, who told the most amazing stories, one who could not just remember where we were, or who I was, but also every book he'd ever read.

AUTHOR BIOGRAPHIES & STORY NOTES

EMMA M BOKALDERE Emma is a Swedish American Latvian living in Oxford. She enjoys long walks, scribbling in her notebook and cuddling cats, allergies be damned.

On 'The Moth': *"I thought I might best put the twist to use through horror, so I implemented something that frightens me — the realisation that a space you thought was safe poses danger. A repetitive dream setting seemed fitting, providing a hazy quality and upping the stakes."*

F E BRADBURY Fi worked as a children's librarian before beginning work in publishing. She works at a literary consultancy in Oxford.

On 'Glass slippers': *"This tale's twist stems from the 'wrong' outcome of a fairy tale relationship, creating ideas within a Cinderella framework that anticipates a happy ending, and pondering, instead, whether its servant-heroine will be forsaking one 'servitude' for another, whether she first needs to cultivate her own autonomy before happiness is attainable."*

HANNAH DADE Hannah writes words and paints pictures. A lover of fantasy and all things magical, she draws from her background in conservation, mental health, linguistics and healthcare policy. She wrote for the website Herstory Arc, and used to work writing letters, then policy, and now works with numbers which are altogether better behaved.

On 'Love in the Leaves': *"This is a story of maternal love for all creatures. The twist occurs within the perspective, rather than the narrative. I took inspiration from nature writers, from the sense that the land is not a thing but a process, and that the earth itself feels."*

MEGAN DAVIS Megan has been in and around Oxford for most of her life. As a place of many great fantastical worlds, she hopes to one day make her literary mark on the city too, even if it's just a small scratch.

On 'My Love, My Life': *"The idea for a retelling of this Greek myth came to me as soon as twisted love stories was suggested as a theme. It is a tragic and warped depiction of self-love."*

'DOC' DAVID *Service of All the Dead*, an early episode of *Inspector Morse*, had this author thinking that Oxford looked like a nice place to be. Years later he finds himself living here.

On 'Leave, leave faire Bride, your solitary bed': *"My story was inspired by a dream in which the Ormskirk Writing Circle go on a trip to Wales. The dream had a beginning, a middle and an end. I was pleased. I thought I had the story. What I ended up with — the story in this book — is nothing like it."*

RICHARD EDWARDS Richard — or Rich to the lazy and extremely busy alike — is from somewhere near Newcastle. After moving south he feels like he's trapped in *Pygmalion*.

On 'Lighthouse Rock': *"The first thing that came to mind when I heard the word 'twist' was a lighthouse. From there, a small world began to take shape — a lonely lighthouse keeper, a harried official who's made a terrible mistake, and two oncoming ships."*

KEVIN ELLIOTT Kevin has tried to escape Oxford for the last twenty years; current plans involve an Irish passport and honing his writing skills. Under no account should you google the phrase 'Kevin Weakest Link'.

On 'Go When the Light Turns Red': *"Progress means more than uncovering facts; the right questions need to be asked. In a world where a single mistake will leave you without air can three people think quickly enough to avoid disaster? And can talent in one area help you elsewhere?"*

GERLINDE Gerlinde is a Belgian illustrator with tons of creative projects that she never seems to find the time to finish (currently including two children's books and three graphic novels). A few years ago she started making autobiographical comic strips which mainly focus on the antics of her boyfriend Thomas. < www.thomaszijnstrip.com >

JESS HYSLOP Jess conserves books by day and writes them by night. A lifetime devotee of speculative fiction, her short stories have appeared in venues such as *Interzone* and *Daily Science Fiction*. She is currently working on a fantasy novel.

On 'Mute': *"If the traditional romance story is about declaring love to our partners, 'Mute' is about the things we don't say: the things we ignore, the things we tolerate in silence, the things we sweep under the rug. With 'Mute', I decided to take this to an extreme."*

JUDE JONES Jude likes anything a bit weird, a bit modern, or a bit pulpy. Her work has appeared in *Jupiter SF Magazine*, previous OWC anthologies, and she was the winner of the Writers in Oxford Short Story prize in 2017.

On 'Buzzing': *"I've never been a fan of the old 'boy meets girl' narratives you see in romantic stories, so I set out to write a story that involves some of the tropes of dating today. It's fairly pessimistic, but then that is the feeling you get after a few hours on Tinder."*

SARAH MILNE DAS   Sarah writes, a fact for which she credits the Oxford Writing Circle. You can find her work in *Longshot Island*, the *Sandspout* and previous OWC anthologies *Debut* and *Oxford's Haunted*. Upcoming in 2018, she is featured in *Wild Musette* and the anthology *Write to Meow*.

On 'What a trifle is a heart': *"The heart is both a physical organ and a rich, well-used metaphor for all kinds of love. I was interested in exploiting that duality by telling a story that's all about feelings, using the most tactile and physically visceral imagery possible. It's a nonsensical distinction, of course — the physical and the emotional bleed into (pun intended!) each other in all of us."*

ELAINE ROBERTS   Elaine works as a marketer in academic publishing and has a BA in English Literature. She loves travel, good food and writing short stories. Often found staring out of the window.

On 'The Three Most Important Words': *"The idea comes from the notion that love is multi-faceted: being in love can be both wonderful and terrible, both joyful and jealousy-inducing. Unfortunately, none of my characters undergo anything so complex. Because when you throw in an audience, love becomes a performance above all else."*

ASHLEY THORPE   Ashley runs a creative writing group at his employer, Oxford University Press. He was shortlisted for Penguin Random House's 'Write-Now' programme in 2016, loves writing various kinds of fiction, and walking the dog. Dislikes: dogs, writing biographies.

On 'Flowers': "*This piece was written as a response to a prompt. The prompt words were 'Clouds, Transparency, Bluebells.' I'd read an article about Spanish bluebells spreading in England earlier in the year, and my initial love story idea came from that. However, the piece ended up going a completely different way...*"

ABIGAIL VINT Abigail is a professional writer and storytelling enthusiast. Her story 'When Invisibles Collide' appeared in the Oxford Writing Circle's *Oxford's Haunted*. She lives in Oxford with her partner Dave and can be found writing in her spare time, mostly in cafés and pubs with other like-minded word nerds.

On 'Shared Interests': "*The story explores the deep emotion we can feel about someone new, at the same time demonstrating how we can easily be swayed by others' perceptions. It is when we mistrust our own instincts that we can break our own hearts.*"

ALEXANDER WALKER Alex has been in Oxford for six years and now considers himself a local. You can find him in his natural habitat of George Street Social, reading, writing or playing board games.

On 'The Memoralabe': "*This story came to life as I begin to journal my own life, keeping track of memories and moments that are important to me. While many do this with the best of intentions, this asks if there is a cost to keeping such details.*"

LYNDSAY WHEBLE Lyndsay Wheble's work has appeared in *Litro*, *Queen Mob's Teahouse*, *DNA Magazine* and on the Yeovil and HISSAC Prize shortlists. She is currently studying for an MA in Creative Writing at Oxford Brookes.

On 'Mrs. Nick Carmichael': "*This piece was inspired by my*

own recollection of the intimacy and violence of school-age female friendships. I remember feeling that social ruin was just one errant remark, or Freudian slip, away, and that my own secrets weighed much heavier than everyone else's."

TIFFANY WILLIAMS Tiffany is a writer whose perfect day begins and ends with reading. She grew up in Oxford and is now enjoying seeing new sides of it as an adult. OWC, being a circle, encompasses many of those sides.

On 'The Violinist': *"This story began in response to a prompt for a feedback session, and when I missed the deadline I took the chance to expand the story. These characters aren't writers, but they've been through something many writers understand; they've lost time for something that once meant a lot to them."*

ABOUT THE OXFORD WRITING CIRCLE

The Oxford Writing Circle is one of Oxford's largest and most vibrant writing communities. Its aim is simple: to encourage more people to write because through writing you can make anything. The group organises weekly events, including sessions to gain feedback on current projects, live writing workshops, guest speakers, and socials.

Find out more at < oxfordwritingcircle.org.uk > and on Meetup.